BANISHED
from the
HERO'S
PARTY,
I Decided to Live a Quiet Life
in the Countryside

3

ZAPPON

Illustration by
Yasumo

"Welcome to my humble little pond. It is a pleasure to have you, Red. And you as well, Rit."

Undine

CONTENTS

Prologue **A Green Hill and the Girl Before She Became the Hero**
001

Chapter 1 **A Peaceful, Slow Life**
005

Chapter 2 **The Hero, Just One Step Away**
033

Chapter 3 **The Hero Wept**
089

Interlude **A Story from an Alternate Universe**
153

Chapter 4 **Heroes Gather in Zoltan**
165

Epilogue **The Sage's Decision**
189

- -

Afterword
197

Illustration: Yasumo
Design Work: Shindousha

"Ooooh, there's so much! It looks **delicious**!"

"Let's make a beef stew, then. Maybe some onions, cabbage, turnips, and leeks for vegetables?"

BANISHED FROM THE HERO'S PARTY,

I Decided to Live a Quiet Life in the Countryside

3

ZAPPON

Illustration by
Yasumo

YEN ON

New York

Banished from the Hero's Party, I Decided to Live a Quiet Life in the Countryside, Vol. 3
Zappon

Translation by Dale DeLucia
Cover art by Yasumo

▼ ▼

SHIN NO NAKAMA JYANAI TO YUUSHA NO PARTY WO OIDASARETANODE, HENKYOU DE SLOW—LIFE SURUKOTO NI SHIMASHITA Vol. 3
©Zappon, Yasumo 2019
First published in Japan in 2019 by KADOKAWA CORPORATION, Tokyo.
English translation rights arranged with KADOKAWA CORPORATION, Tokyo through TUTTLE-MORI AGENCY, INC., Tokyo.

English translation © 2021 by Yen Press, LLC

Yen On
150 West 30th Street, 19th Floor
New York, NY 10001

Visit us at yenpress.com
facebook.com/yenpress
twitter.com/yenpress
yenpress.tumblr.com
instagram.com/yenpress

First Yen On Edition: May 2021

Yen On is an imprint of Yen Press, LLC.
The Yen On name and logo are trademarks of Yen Press, LLC.

▼ ▼

Library of Congress Cataloging-in-Publication Data
Names: Zappon, author. | Yasumo, illustrator. | DeLucia, Dale, translator.
Title: Banished from the hero's party, I decided to live a quiet life in the countryside / Zappon ; illustration by Yasumo ; translation by Dale DeLucia ; cover art by Yasumo.
Other titles: Shin no nakama ja nai to yuusha no party wo oidasareta node, henkyou de slow life suru koto ni shimashita. English
Description: First Yen On edition. | New York : Yen On, 2020.
Identifiers: LCCN 2020026847 | ISBN 9781975312459 (v. 1 ; trade paperback) | ISBN 9781975312473 (v. 2 ; trade paperback) | ISBN 9781975312497 (v. 3 ; trade paperback)
Subjects: CYAC: Ability—Fiction. | Fantasy.
Classification: LCC PZ7.1.Z37 Ban 2020 | DDC [Fic]—dc23
LC record available at https://lccn.loc.gov/2020026847

ISBNs: 978-1-9753-1249-7 (paperback)
978-1-9753-1250-3 (ebook)

1 3 5 7 9 10 8 6 4 2

LSC-C

Printed in the United States of America

CHARACTERS

Red
(Gideon Ragnason)

Kicked out of the Hero's party, he headed to the frontier to live a slow life. One of humanity's greatest swordsmen with many feats to his name.

Rit
(Rizlet of Loggervia)

The princess of the Duchy of Loggervia. Adventured with Red's party in the past. One thing led to another, and she forced herself into Red's shop and is now living with him. An easily embarrassed girl who has outgrown her more combative phase.

Bui of Maoduester
(Shisandan)

A young man who claims to be a member of an aristocratic family from a country destroyed by the demon lord's forces. He replaced Albert as a B-rank adventurer. In reality, he is Shisandan, a general in the demon lord's army who Red and company once battled.

Ruti Ragnason

Red's younger sister and possessor of the Divine Blessing of the Hero, humanity's strongest blessing. She was extremely attached to her big brother and always clung to him when the two were younger. Before he left the party, Red used to dote on his cute little sister.

Ares Srowa

Bearer of the Divine Blessing of the Sage, greatest of the Mage blessings. The man who pushed Red out of the party. Son of a failed duke, he joined the Hero's party in order to restore his family's power.

Tisse Garland

A young girl with the Divine Blessing of the Assassin, she was brought in by Ares to replace Red. Largely expressionless but has the greatest common sense of anyone in the Hero's party. Keeps a pet spider she named Mister Crawly Wawly.

Theodora Dephilo

The pinnacle of human clerics and assistant instructor of the temple knight's style of spear wielding. Bearer of the Divine Blessing of the Crusader. A warrior at heart, she has a stoic personality. Has a high opinion of Red's abilities.

Danan LeBeau

A big, brawny man with the Divine Blessing of the Martial Artist. Used to be the master of a dojo in a town that was destroyed by the demon lord's army. Despite this, there is no trace of that dark past in his hearty personality.

Albert Leland

The frontier's strongest adventurer. Has the Divine Blessing of the Champion and a strong ambition to move up in the world. Although in the top tier for the frontier, he ended up drifting out to Zoltan after not being able to cut it in Central.

▲ ▲

Prologue

- - - - - - - -

A Green Hill and the Girl Before She Became the Hero

▶ ▲ ▲ ◢ ◀

Cloudless blue skies. A gentle breeze rustled across a verdant hill.

"Big Brother," Ruti called out.

She did not have any armor or weapons equipped. At present, she was just a normal village girl. Atop her pretty blue hair sat a hat accented with a white ribbon.

She had a basket in her hand. Inside was some bread, cheese, a little bit of bacon, and some goat's milk to go with it.

"Shall we go ahead and have lunch now?"

"Yes." Ruti was smiling from her spot sitting next to me. "I'm glad we could spend a whole week together, Big Brother."

I had been stationed at the border region between the Kingdom of Avalonia and the Kingdom of Veronia to the south. Relations had grown strained between the two nations as of late. After finishing my six-month deployment, I had been given a bit of a rest and had come back to see Ruti.

Spending peaceful moments with my little sister was enjoyable. Protecting that smiling little girl was the only reason I'd persevered through the many trials of being a knight.

Even this won't last forever, though.

My Divine Blessing—Guide—had the initial skill of level +30. Other than starting strong, it provided no redeeming features.

When the time came for Ruti to begin her journey, I would protect her from anything, be it orcs, dragons, or something worse. But at some point, I would reach my limit. And when that time came...

Ruti squeezed my hand. Her red eyes were looking straight at me as I glanced back at her in surprise.

"What is it?" I asked.

"You said before that my holding your hand helped you to calm down."

Maybe my worries had been showing on my face. This was a rare moment's peace with Ruti, so I decided to set my consternations aside for now. There would be time for them later.

"Thank you. I feel better now."

"I see. In that case, I'm glad."

I ran a hand through Ruti's hair, and her eyes narrowed a bit as she allowed it. Things were tranquil for a little while, but my mind was quickly beset upon by another concern.

If I worked even harder, would it be possible to spare Ruti from her responsibilities as the Hero? Was there some way to let her enjoy peaceful days like this one forever?

Even I understood that such a dream was far-fetched. There was no way the Hero could go their entire life without doing anything. Still, I wanted my adorable little sister never to know conflict or hardship.

Unsurprisingly, I failed to see that goal realized.

That very same day when I was spending time with Ruti, the demon lord, Taraxon the Wrathful, gave the order, and battleship after battleship carrying his forces from the dark continent landed on the southern beaches of Avalon.

The demon lord's army sent messengers delivering the declaration of war, and the next day they began an all-out assault. In less than half a week, all the coastal cities had surrendered, and by the time the continent's various rulers knew of the declaration of war, the demon lord's army had already gained a strong foothold in Avalon.

Two years later, Taraxon's forces had taken half of Avalon. That's when Ruti's village was attacked, and she rose up as the Hero who would someday crush the demon lord and all who served him. Naturally, I was fighting by her side.

However, by the time we took back our home, that verdant hill we'd visited that one day had long since been burned to a lifeless brown.

Chapter 1

A Peaceful, Slow Life

Mayor Tornado and the higher-ups of the Adventurers Guild had gathered in a room at the Zoltan Assembly.

The last of the stalker demons that fled had been hunted down. After many ups and downs, the Devil's Blessing incident that had caused such a fuss in Zoltan had finally been resolved.

Bui was the one who had slain the demons. He was a swordsman of unknown origin since he had yet to register with the Adventurers Guild. In fact, he was to be the topic of discussion at today's meeting.

"If we believe his statement—which does not currently have any corroboration—he is a wandering noble. However, as the fourth son of his house, he has no inheritance."

"The Maoduester family? Aren't they an aristocratic clan from the Flamberge Kingdom? I thought the demon lord's army had destroyed that country."

"It's not like a noble house disappears simply because their homeland falls. The first wife of the Maoduester family is the daughter of an aristocrat from the Kingdom of Veronia. Apparently, they have been staying there."

"I see. And where did that information come from?"

"Bui's statement."

"So we're back to the question of how much of it is true."

"Does it really matter? Even if Bui was on the run after committing a murder somewhere, I'm not going to look a gift horse in the mouth," Tornado admitted.

Some of the Adventurers Guild leadership furrowed a brow at that, but no one openly objected.

"As a special exception, we'll acknowledge Bui as a C-rank adventurer. If he forms a party and successfully deals with the blade sharks disrupting the fishing grounds to the south, then we'll grant his group B-rank status. After that, he'll have Zoltan's blessing. There aren't any objections."

The gathered committee had approached Rit about coming back, but in the end, she'd turned them down with no room for rebuttal. High-ranking adventurers were a rarity out in the frontier. Master Mistorm, the former mayor of Zoltan, was one, but she was long retired. Another, Moen, was the captain of the guard, and he was still quite busy dealing with the cleanup from all the trouble the Devil's Blessing caused. There was little alternative than to have Bui take Albert's place as the town's B-rank adventurer.

Goran, one of the leaders at the Adventurers Guild who was in line to become mayor after Tornado, was a little bit unreliable, and Tornado was determined to leave a solid footing for Zoltan when his term was up. Master Mistorm had been a brilliant mage, but she hadn't even risen to the level of mediocre when it came to her mayoral responsibilities.

A politician resolving conflicts themselves via combat was the worst possible plan. That sort of strategy wasn't a permanent solution. Master Mistorm had retired, after all. In Tornado's mind, a mayor's role was to establish a system that could smoothly deal with problems without requiring constant intervention from Zoltan's leaders.

"So according to plan, then?"

"Yes, there's no way he would fail against the likes of those blade sharks. Take care of the B-rank approval once he returns. I intend to sell it to the people as the birth of a new hero at the memorial services for the victims of the Devil's Blessing," Mayor Tornado instructed.

In the end, all the meeting had accomplished was deciding to prop up Bui as Zoltan's new B-rank adventurer.

If the enigmatic young nobleman intended to stick around in Zoltan, he might well become mayor himself someday. Undoubtedly, he was the sort of champion that Zoltan could rely on going forward.

* * *

The fields and pastures on the outskirts of Zoltan stretched far into the horizon.

At this time of year, the farmers in northern Zoltan ventured past the two-meter-tall ramparts—really just simple stone walls—that encircled the settlement to gather feed for livestock over the winter. There were already some people from the working-class part of town collecting food for their animals, too.

Because the work offered the chance for a little profit on the side, some D-rank and lower adventurers were participating in the chore as well. While not common, monsters could show up in the fields, so it was handy to have battle-ready people around. Any adventurer who volunteered was welcomed, and there was no established maximum on participants.

The remuneration wasn't much, but because the farmers would share some of their vegetables, wheat, or other foodstuffs, the task was popular among the poorer adventurers and those for whom adventuring was a secondary job. Admittedly, even medicinal herb gathering was more profitable. This job was safer, however. If you got hurt, there were plenty of people around who could carry you back to town. Simple, non-life-threatening work was appealing.

All the gathered grass was to be stored in barns on the north side of Zoltan. Come winter, it would be processed into hay and sold at a fair price.

"Feels like the cold's already on its way."

The sky was beautiful and clear, and the temperature was just a little bit cool.

I was wearing a coat over my usual shirt. Clutching a bundle of cheese and potatoes I had received from a farmer in exchange for some medicine in my right hand, I made my way back home. The farmer had even been kind enough to throw in some chestnuts.

"This is still warm compared to Loggervia," Rit replied as she stuck her hand into my coat pocket. She wrapped her fingers around mine in an attempt to shake the chill from hers.

"I thought it was still warm?"

"Comparatively. It's still winter."

Perhaps a little embarrassed, Rit raised the bandanna around her neck just a little bit to cover her mouth.

Squeezing her hand back, I caught a glimpse of her breaking into a smile behind her kerchief. It was so cute I couldn't help but smirk.

"Look at that grin," Rit teased.

It hardly seemed fair that she could tease me when she was doing the same thing, but I kept quiet.

We got back to the shop before noon, still a bit early for lunch.

Rit pulled the three ten-liter bottles of milk we had gotten from another farmer out of her item box with its extra-dimensional storage.

You might think we could have put the bag I was carrying in the item box, too, but while the item box recognized a bottle of milk as a singular item, it didn't acknowledge a bag of potatoes as such. Each spud would be stowed separately. Taking them out would require removing each potato and each piece of cheese one by one. You also had to memorize what every individual vegetable looked like when you dropped it in, which was pretty annoying. If a bushel could just be carried in a regular bag, that was generally quicker.

"If we don't use all this milk soon, it'll spoil."

"Maybe take one to the market and exchange it for something else?"

"Yeah, I'll be right back, then."

"Can I come, too?"

"Of course."

Now, if both Rit and I were continually popping out, it raised the question of who would tend the shop. If only we had someone else to hold down the fort. But fall was drawing to a close, and the two of us wanted to go for a stroll. What were we supposed to do? If Gonz heard me making excuses like that, he'd probably have a good laugh. Thankfully, there was no one here but Rit and me, and I intended to make the most of our quiet life.

I grabbed a bag of bronze commons before Rit and I headed back out.

Zoltan's summer listlessness was nowhere to be found at the market anymore. Shopkeepers were bundled up, and they were all aggressively calling for customers. They were doing everything they could to unload their inventories.

"So what shall we get?"

At markets in Avalon, it was possible to make purchases with cash, but there was also a lot of bartering. A bronze common, worth one-hundredth of a payril, was often used as a proxy for haggling. In some farming villages, this wound up making the less valuable coins the main currency in circulation instead of the more precious silver payril.

Such was the case at Dr. Newman's clinic a while back. An elderly lady had settled her fee with some commons and a bit of meat. That sort of practice was regular all over the continent.

From what I'd heard, the dark continent had continued down the path to developing a currency-based economy. Unlike here, where self-cast coins were mixed in among the official money, they only used bronze coins that bore an official seal.

Before the war, there were countries in Avalon that had imported currency from the dark continent to use as their national money because the dark continent's coins had a stable value and were of a higher quality.

If you were ever going to go to the dark continent, it was a good idea to exchange your currency in one of those nations.

The price of dairy was a bit high in Zoltan. Cows were better suited to slightly cooler climates, so milk cost about twenty percent more than in Central. Typically, ten liters ran you about five payril, but it cost six in Zoltan, which would cover about six days' worth of living expenses. Thus, instead of trading the entire bottle of milk all in one place, we would probably end up bartering off portions of it for ingredients from a few shops. The other option was to trade it all away for something expensive that Rit and I otherwise wouldn't usually indulge in.

While dairy was pricey in Zoltan, beef was cheaper than average. A farmer had mentioned that the climate here was better suited for raising beef cattle, but the price for meat wasn't much lower than in Central. If you were lucky, you could get it for around five percent less—roughly 4.5 payril per kilogram. Something about that didn't feel right to me.

"It's starting to be about time for stews, isn't it?" Rit mentioned.

"A stew, huh? What do you think about getting some sausage for a pot-au-feu?" I proposed.

"Would it be okay to just get some beef for it? I like stewed beef!"

"That would be good. Maybe some onions, cabbage, turnips, and leeks for vegetables? A marinated fish for an appetizer. And some fried chicken to go along with the hot pot. We can put some pasta in to finish things off when the hot pot is ready, too. I'll get some yogurt and fruit for dessert."

"Ooooh, that sounds amazing! But is that really okay? It's not like this is a special occasion or anything." Rit looked a little bit unsure, though her eyes were gleaming at my proposed menu.

I just brushed it off with a smile. It was too embarrassing to admit that I'd gotten so enthusiastic because Rit had asked for a specific dish.

✳   ✳   ✳

"It's ready."

"Oooooh!"

I placed the pot on the stand set up on top of the table in the living room. Then I put a single piece of charcoal in the burner and lit it up.

It wasn't an especially powerful flame, but the pot was already plenty heated, so the charcoal's addition caused it to start bubbling.

"Shall we, then?"

"Yeah."

There was hardly anything left of the marinated fish we had eaten while preparing the hot pot. I was a little worried it was a bit too much as an appetizer, but with the hot pot sitting in front of us, it became clear that my concerns had been unfounded. Neither Rit nor I slowed down in the slightest as we partook of the stew.

We had fun chatting as we kept picking away at the hot pot.

"These chicken meatballs are delicious."

"They really are. That old guy at the butcher's shop recommended them so highly that I had to give them a try. He was right. They go well with the beef. I'll have to remember to thank him later."

When we finished, we added the pasta and let it simmer. Combining the noodles with broth that had absorbed all of the ingredients' flavors was fantastic. For dessert, we had yogurt with grapes and sliced bananas mixed in.

Rit, who loved sweet things, seemed to be in heaven as she ate. It almost made me want to share my portion with her.

But— Well, I ended up eating my dessert myself. I mean, I liked sweet things, too.

"Thanks for the meal!"

When, at last, our feast was complete, Rit had a broad, satisfied smile. The mere sight of it was enough to make me glad that I'd prepared such an extravagant meal.

In the afternoon, we were back to working in the store. I left the counter to Rit and went into the workshop to prepare antidotes using gray starfish grass.

The Devil's Blessing's production base was gone, but there was no telling whether the authorities had found all the existing stock yet. Treatments for withdrawal were still ongoing, too. There was going to be a demand for a curative that helped manage those symptoms.

"They're probably going to need to start mass-producing Cure Poison potions, aren't they?"

Magic interpreted the effects of medication overdose as a toxin, so by using Cure Poison, it was possible to instantly heal the physical ailments of prolonged use and overdose. It couldn't do anything about the psychological effects of addiction, however. The larger issue was that Cure Poison potions were quite expensive, costing around three hundred payril each. So only wealthy adventurers, merchants, or aristocrats could get their hands on them.

"It would be nice if an herb-based concoction could provide a more affordable option," I muttered to myself.

Unfortunately, the antidotes I could make using plants were only capable of mitigating the symptoms slightly.

A Cure Poison potion was a magic mixture made by infusing a spell into a tincture. I couldn't use magic, so I couldn't make it.

I could use my multiplying potion to turn one Cure Poison brew into five and sell them at a lower price, but...

"If there was only someone I could trust to keep a secret and had enough influence to get it out into circulation..."

Most of the people I knew in Zoltan were working-class folks. I didn't have any particularly powerful connections.

"Well, if that route's no good, then there's no need to worry about it," I decided.

It wasn't like people were going to die without a Cure Poison potion.

The only problem was that the holy church had judged the act of using Devil's Blessing as blasphemy. So, while the organization would typically have taken the lead in providing for those in need, they were currently refraining from rendering any assistance.

In order to care for someone who was suffering from withdrawal symptoms, the person needed a partner to nurse them until the medicine was entirely out of their system. There were several clinics in

Zoltan, but there was not very much capacity for inpatient care. By and large, the clinics just healed the people who stopped in, and any stays were for very short spells, followed by home care.

"Either way, it's too big of a problem for me to tackle myself."

There were all sorts of things to consider, and it wasn't the kind of issue that was going to have an easy resolution.

All I could give was my best as an apothecary.

That evening, when I was mostly done with the preparations, I headed out to the shop to see how things were going. There I saw Rit smiling at me from the counter.

It looked like business had been good today.

"Because of the riot in Southmarsh, we've sold a lot of 'just in case' sorts of medicines, like the hemostatics. Also, the guards bought quite a lot of the hangover cures. And we managed to clear out a few cure potions, too."

We'd paid some local adventurers to help with making those cure potions. Rit and I had spent a flat thirteen payril for the concoctions. While a time-consuming task for a fledgling adventurer, it was a popular job regardless, as it was an easy source of good income. All it took was casting some magic.

"Oh, that's amazing. This might be our most profitable day in a long while."

"It's definitely in our top two. And we were only open in the afternoon today. Also, apparently, every clinic in town is running low on medicine, so expect some orders soon."

Rit handed me a memo with today's transaction records scribbled on it. I skimmed it quickly. We had definitely done an impressive amount of business.

"In that case, I should prepare a bit more medicine for tomorrow. I guess I'll have to work a little bit longer today."

"It might be a good idea to keep the store open today until customers stop coming, too," Rit suggested.

"That would mean a bit of overtime work for you. Do you mind?"

"Not at all! I think we've been attracting some new customers recently, so let's show them the high quality that Red & Rit's Apothecary has to offer."

"Quality," huh? I was a tiny bit uneasy for my work to be the subject of such high praise, but I did pride myself on not selling medicines that had been mis-prepared. And we hadn't ever had any complaints from customers.

I had no chance trying to compete on price with a shop run by someone with a blessing that could make curatives using Intermediate Preparation or a person who could use spells to make magic potions. Still, not every customer was looking for such high-class items.

"This cold medicine, please!" a small, half-elf girl chirped as she handed over ten commons.

It was a medicine that used ginger to increase the body's metabolism. Unlike a drug made using a skill, it did not immediately take effect, but slower-acting compounds had their uses, too.

"Be careful not to drop it," Rit cautioned with a smile as she handed over the requested item.

"Thank you! My mom caught a cold and was feeling really bad!"

"I'm sure she'll feel better soon."

The little girl politely nodded and then left the store with a spring in her step.

I'm Tisse. I used to be an assassin, but now I'm more like an airship pilot.

The Hero and I are currently headed toward Zoltan in a flying vessel left behind by the previous demon lord who had been resting deep within some desert ruins. The Hero was searching for an alchemist capable of creating something called Devil's Blessing, a drug she learned about after interrogating a demon.

The demon had spread the medicine all around Zoltan, so there was no doubt that there was someone capable of making Devil's Blessing there. Moments ago, lights from Zoltan homes had become visible in the distance.

Night fell, and I landed the airship near a forest a ways off from the road so I could rest.

"We will arrive tomorrow."

I had unfurled a map and was explaining the route we would take.

"Okay."

The Hero quietly listened as I spoke while gesturing to the map.

Occasionally, she would look at me, and her cheek would twitch a little. It startled me and made me wonder if I had done something that upset her. However, whenever it happened, Mister Crawly Wawly would tap my shoulder with his leg, as if to say "There, there," and cheer me up.

He's right. I can do this! Eeep?! She twitched again! She's looking straight at me! It's okay. Stay calm. Stay calm…

"Land here tomorrow," the Hero instructed as she pointed at the map.

It was a point near a mountain about a day's walk from Zoltan.

"Are you sure? Zoltan is a bit of a long way off from there."

"The airship draws attention. I want to hide the fact that I'm the Hero while in Zoltan. You should treat me as just a normal traveler, too."

What?! Nowaynowaynowaynowaynoway!

I mean, leaving the airship far away was fine, and walking that far was okay, too! But there was no way the Hero could pass as an average person!

Just standing next to her got me so nervous that I was like a cold sweat waterfall! My back was soaked! I had to wash my underwear every night from the sweat!

Someone with such an overwhelming "I'm the strongest around" sort of aura like hers could only be either the Hero or the demon lord! Not that I'd ever met the demon lord, though.

"I see," I finally managed. "It might be a bit presumptuous of me to bring this up, but you don't seem to be particularly familiar with normal travel..."

"That's correct. Everywhere I've visited, it's always been as the Hero. That's why I would like your help to cover for me if I make any mistakes while trying to pass as a regular traveler."

Are you serious?

"I'm not sure I'm fit to be your guide here. I am but a lowly assassin."

"That's beside the point. Just a moment ago, you were willing to point out my lack of familiarity with normal excursions."

Wait—that got me high marks? Anyone could have pointed that much out.

Getting into an argument with the Hero was frightening in its own way, so I had no choice but to concede. It was an assassin's job to respond as capably as possible to her employer's requests, after all.

At least I had been trained on blending into crowds, and as for the Hero...well, that was going to be hopeless. Still, I couldn't say that to her. I was content to nod and live to see another day.

Surviving hardship was crucial in my line of work.

"All right, those are the plans for tomorrow, then. You can rest now. I'll keep watch." And with that, the Hero went out on the deck.

My name is Tisse. I used to be an assassin and an airship pilot, but now my duty is to support the Hero as she disguises herself as an inconspicuous traveler. I could never have imagined this situation back when I was an assassin.

Seriously, I literally couldn't have conceived of something so crazy.

That night, while I was washing my sweat-soaked underwear, I sensed that the Hero was up and walking around. My ears perked up.

"...No one."

She almost sounded dejected. "No one?" I mean, yeah, we were the only two on the airship, so of course no one else was around. I

wondered what she was doing. Mister Crawly Wawly tilted his head as
if to say he didn't know, either.

*   *   *

Zoltan had a subtropical climate, but on days when the winds blew
down from the big mountain range that ran along the eastern
border—the Wall at the End of the World—it felt quite a bit colder.

As Rit and I were getting ready to open the shop that morning, she
shivered when the wind blew in.

"Should I close the window? It's a cold one today."

"Yes, please do."

Apparently, the winter in Zoltan was even chilly for Rit, raised in
the northern country of Loggervia.

I closed the wooden window and then lit a lamp to keep the room
from being too dark. The faint scent of the burning oil and the lan-
tern's dim light filled the shop.

"Okay, let's do our best today, too."

"You bet."

Rit and I high-fived, and then I flipped the sign on the front door to
OPEN FOR BUSINESS.

As I turned to go back into the shop, a frigid wind whistled as it
surged by.

"Whew, that's cold. But being able to go into your home when you're
chilly is bliss."

Trudging on and on to continue a journey that had to persist no
matter what. Enduring an icy wind coursing over the vast plains with
just a cloak and without any trees around to take refuge behind. The
armor encasing your body freezes over. Your ears, fingers, and every
other extremity aches and burns. And amid all that, being stalked
from afar by starved monsters eyeing a rare prey that would attack at a
moment's notice if you showed even the slightest opening.

Unlike when that had been my daily life, now, if it was cold outside,

I could just go back into my cozy home, and Rit would wrap my blue hands in hers to warm them up.

"Eh-heh-heh."

Rit flashed an embarrassed smile as she held my hands. I smiled, too, feeling my own face getting a little bit red as I did so.

These were happy days.

This slow and easy life of ours had admittedly dulled our danger senses, however.

"Heeey! Let me in to warm up a bit...!" Gonz called as he barged in.

Rit and I were a split second too slow in reacting to the half-elf carpenter. Seeing our hands together as we looked into each other's eyes like that, Gonz looked surprised for a moment, and then his mouth cracked into a grin.

We frantically pulled away from each other, and Rit blushed as she announced, "I'm going to go organize the storage room!" before beating a quick retreat.

"My bad, my bad. Didn't mean to ruin the moment. But you did have the open sign out on the door."

"Yeah, I guess so..."

"What's there to be so embarrassed about anyway? The whole neighborhood already knows you two are lovey-dovey. You're pretty much always at it. Ain't it a bit late to be getting flustered now?"

"Huh? Are we really that lovey-dovey?" I wondered aloud.

"Huh?" Gonz's eyes went wide, as if he couldn't believe the words coming out of my mouth. And then he heaved a big sigh.

"I mean, yeah, pretty much everyone agrees you two are the most stupidly in-love couple in all of Zoltan."

Ugh, does everyone really think of us like that?

Truthfully, I had been restraining myself. Honestly, I would have liked to have been even more intimate with Rit.

"Well, whatever. So what did you want?" Though not in the smoothest way, I shifted the topic of conversation.

"Nothing in particular. Just what you said back at the shop's opening. 'Feel free to stop by for some tea' and all. I could use some warm tea."

"All right, I'll get right on that, so watch the shop a bit for me."

"Leave it to me."

I headed to the kitchen, chuckling to myself as Gonz stood behind the counter in his work clothes, pointlessly swinging his arm.

I prepared the tea with practiced ease, placing three cups with white steam rising out of them onto a tray and heading back out to the store. No customers had stopped by.

Rit had come back before me, having already regained her composure. She was sitting at the counter.

"Ahhh, that hits the spot." Gonz groaned with satisfaction.

"Whoa now, you've still got work to do, don't you?" I chided.

"Yeah, but my work's outside. It gets rough this time of year."

"Isn't the summer heat worse?"

"Sure, but winter's bad enough in its own right! It's a different kind of difficult!"

The two of us laughed as Gonz stressed the point. Still, I could understand what he was saying. Winter and summer were both pretty harsh.

"It's the fingertips in particular."

Gonz rubbed his slender, pale, un-carpenter-like digits together. An accident had left him with a broken finger years ago, but elves possessed a tenacious sort of life force. The snapped bone had healed on its own without leaving so much as a scar.

I liked Rit's hands more, however, with their calluses and blemishes from all her fights and training. They were all the more endearing because you could see everything she had gone through to get here.

"Oy. Why'd you suddenly grab your lady's hand?"

"Ah, it just sort of happened."

Gonz shrugged, looking more and more exasperated. Rit was blushing as she hid a grin behind her bandanna. She was looking cuter and cuter.

"All right already. I get it. Thanks for the tea. If I stay any longer, I'm going to vomit pure sugar, so I should be on my way."

"Okay. Don't hurt yourself out there."

"I'll do my best."

Gonz finished off the remaining tea in one gulp, put his gloves back on, and ventured into the chilly air.

"Gonz looked cold," Rit remarked.

"It must be hard working outside on a day like this."

Still sipping our tea, Rit and I were filled with a sort of detached respect as we watched our friend soldier off to resume construction on a house.

Winter was not just someone else's problem as far as Red & Rit's Apothecary was concerned.

✳   ✳   ✳

"Not a single customer."

No one came by today.

I was resting my chin on my hand, absentmindedly passing the time.

"I made some coffee, so let's take a little break," Rit said.

A short reprieve was probably fine. It wasn't like we were going to get busy out of nowhere suddenly. My shoulders slumped a bit as I headed over to Rit. Seeing that, she smiled wryly.

"It's just one day without any patrons. You don't have to get so down about it."

Yesterday had been one of our best business days ever. I'd prepared lots of medicines in excited preparation for that trend to continue, but the store was so empty I could hear crickets.

"Selling all those drugs yesterday means that everyone's got what they need for now. There's an ebb and flow to it," Rit said soothingly.

"Maybe, but still..."

Typically, there were lots of people picking up medicinal cookies before work, but today we hadn't sold one—they were all still sitting in their basket. They had been based on a recipe I had for preserved food, so they didn't have to be disposed of after a single day, but it was depressing seeing things I had made lying around there like that.

"I would have thought it would get a bit warmer in the afternoon," Rit remarked as she opened the window a little, letting a cold wind blow through the shop. "But yeah, with it this cold, Zoltanis aren't going to be in a hurry to go walking around outside."

One of the mottos around here was "It'll wait till tomorrow." Whether it was hot, cold, or rainy, any day that it was annoying to do something, people would take care of the bare minimum and procrastinate on the other stuff.

I'd gotten used to that Zoltan way of things, and it's not as though I despised it, but…

"When it gets even colder, customers are going to be fewer and farther between," I sighed.

Rit patted my head to console me.

Having someone you love do that for you was comforting. It was great when you were feeling down.

"You just need to have some kind of product that will draw them in because of the chill," Rit reasoned.

"There are magic potions that grant cold resistance, but those are expensive at five hundred payril a bottle, and they only last a minute, so they won't be any good for us."

The concoction was more for surviving intense, conjured frost that would kill you instantly. There weren't any potions for enduring an entire winter's day.

The reason was that it was challenging to maintain magic for an extended period. With a Preparation skill, you could make medicines with longer-lasting effects like inner fire tablets that raised your body temperature or the dunce wonder pill that decreased intelligence. However, they were for emergencies only and had deleterious effects on the body when taken regularly.

"Yeah, this is a tough one to solve."

Rit shifted up a gear from patting my head to pulling it to rest on her shoulder and rubbing from the back of my head to my neck as she struggled to come up with a solution.

"If only common skills were enough to make a Loggervian heater."

"Hmm."

Oh yeah...

I had totally forgotten about those.

Loggervian heaters were a device created in the Duchy of Loggervia. They used iron powder, saline water, a fine powder of charcoal from Loggervian cedar, and some breadcrumbs. One could use an Intermediate Alchemy skill to combine those reagents into a packet that gave off heat.

Initially, they had been a national secret and distributed only to their soldiers, but during the upheaval the goblin king caused fifty years ago, Loggervia had shared the preparation method with its neighbors. In the cold north, the use of Loggervian heaters to keep soldiers warm led to a marked increase in morale and an improved ability to sustain combat.

At present, the little tools were quite widespread among the northern regions of Avalon. Still, despite their convenience and the cheap ingredients needed to craft them, they weren't something that everyone used. The biggest reason for this was that they started giving off warmth as soon as they were assembled. That meant they needed to be given to the user immediately. Intermediate Alchemy was required to craft Loggervian heaters, making it difficult for travelers to get their hands on the items.

"They would be perfect for an apothecary to sell in the morning," I said.

"They need Intermediate Alchemy, though, right? That's what I heard at a store in Loggervia, at least," Rit replied.

"Heh-heh-heh... The truth is I discovered a different recipe during my travels."

"This is an old Loggervian national secret we're talking about here." Rit looked shocked as she tousled my hair.

Even among alchemists, not many people investigated how exactly alchemy skills functioned. That was because such research demanded proper know-how instead of relying on a skill, and it was challenging to gain that knowledge. But because I had looked into ways to lessen the impulses of Ruti's blessing, I had learned in detail how exactly those skills functioned. My old efforts were still paying off.

I never did find any way to lessen the impulses of a blessing with as many powerful immunities and resistances as the Hero, though, which was what I had been looking for.

"For Loggervian heaters, apparently what the Intermediate Alchemy skill actually does is interact with the iron powder and charcoal. The rest of it can be done with Elementary Alchemy or no skill at all. The warming effect comes from the iron powder oxidizing. Everything else in the recipe is just to facilitate that process."

Loggervia was known for its iron production, supported by the abundance of high-quality lumber it boasted. An alchemist who was native to the region and well versed in reactions involving iron had discovered the formula for the heaters.

"Which means that all you need to do is make the iron powder rust extremely quickly. In which case, if you use the extract of a rust-eating mushroom, the process should be even more efficient. And if you use iron powder, a diluted solution of the mushroom extract, and bread crumbs, then Loggervian heaters can be made with common skills."

The party's travels through cold lands had been so much more comfortable after I'd discovered that recipe.

"I don't really know much about Alchemy skills, but isn't that kind of insanely amazing...?" Rit asked.

When I'd told the Hero's party about my discovery way back when, they had responded with blank stares. Not only were they all strong and sturdy, but their minds focused more on things that were useful in combat. It was a journey to defeat the demon lord, so I could hardly blame them. The party likely could have endured any climate if they'd just put their mind to it.

It may not have felt like much of an achievement in the past, but Rit complimenting me for my discovery now made me elated.

"So…how about that?" I asked hesitantly.

"How about what?" Rit replied, confused.

"Is there going to be a problem if we start selling these? I don't want a multiplying potion issue on our hands."

Rit hugged me tight and pressed her forehead to mine with a laugh. "This will be okay. This is sure to let everyone know just how amazing you are."

"Phew."

"Seriously, though…my Red is really something," Rit said happily, then flashed a dazzling smile.

This time, she didn't cover her mouth with her bandanna, letting her happiness show.

"It's because you're always there for me," I answered as I hugged Rit back.

I got the blacksmith Mogrim to give me some iron powder and put together some samples. Leaving the store to Rit, I headed to where Gonz was working.

"Hey, Gonz."

"Oh, that you, Red? Pretty rare to see you out and about."

Today Gonz was building a new warehouse for a clothing shop. The support pillars were already up, and he was working on the walls. His long half-elf ears were red, affected even more than most by the winter cold. He had a wool scarf wrapped around his neck, but in general, he was wearing lighter clothes that wouldn't get in the way of his work.

"It's a cold one today," Gonz observed as he pulled off his leather work gloves and put his hands on his ears to warm them up. His nose and head had turned a cherry color, too, and he looked like he was suffering.

"I brought a sample for you to try out."

"A sample?"

"Yeah, it's for cold days like today. It's a heater."

I pulled one of the heaters in a pouch out of my basket and passed it over to Gonz.

"Whoa, that's pretty warm." Gonz looked to be enjoying it as he held it against his fingers and ears.

"I was thinking about trying to sell them. They should stay warm for somewhere around fifteen hours."

"Seriously? I would definitely want one!"

Gonz had already snatched up the Loggervian heater I'd offered him, claiming it for himself, which caused me to chuckle a little.

"What do you got there?"

Tanta's father, Mido, and some other craftspeople stopped working and crowded around.

"I made a bunch, so there's enough for everyone."

I passed the heaters to the laborers one after another.

"Oooh, that's warm."

"I really hate the cold."

"Damn, this is nice."

The response was excellent. I made certain to explain the general warnings for use, so they didn't burn themselves or anything.

"And these should still be warm in the evening, so if you don't mind, could you spread the word about them at the tavern when you go home?"

"But there ain't no way this won't cost an arm and a leg, right?" a half-orc craftsman joked.

Grinning, I responded, "For the low, low price of just a single quarter payril, you get one of these and five coppers change."

"The price o' two whiskeys, eh? I can just write it off as the cost of the drinks I'd normally get to warm up!"

"But you're still gonna drink, right? Don't go hurting yourself working while you're drunk."

"If I do, I'll be countin' on you for some good drugs."

"If you get yourself hurt for such a stupid reason, I'll be sure to charge you through the nose for the medicine."

The crafters all burst out laughing.

When people warmed up, their moods melted with them. The crafters seemed to be in high spirits as they went back to work.

I left them to their duties and went off to visit Stormthunder at his furniture shop, the various delivery people, Dr. Newman and his nurse, Eleanora, out doing house calls, the dwarf Grihardr repairing a pot by the fireside, the high elf Oparara pulling her food cart, and many others.

My last stop was Mogrim's place. I wanted to give him a heater as thanks and to talk about buying iron powder from him going forward. He just looked amused, but his wife, Mink, who watched the storefront, was interested.

With luck, everyone I gave a sample to would be telling their friends and neighbors about the Loggervian heaters.

"That should be perfect as far as advertisements go."

It wasn't until after I'd finished distributing the pouches that I realized it had already gotten dark. The work had taken a lot longer than I had expected.

Since winter was so short here, I had thought heaters wouldn't be in that high a demand, but everyone seemed really interested. I certainly wasn't ungrateful for the response, but everywhere I went, people wanted to know more about them and when they'd be available to purchase. Some even tried to put in preorders for tomorrow.

"Ugh, so cold."

A cold night breeze blew past as I was walking along a tree-lined path. The moon was gradually growing brighter as the sun sank farther. Several enthusiastic stars were already glimmering.

My white breath melted into the air as the last ray of daylight waned in the sky.

"Red."

Someone called out to me. It was a bright, clear voice that was music to my ears. Looking around, I saw Rit waving.

"Why are you out here?"

"I had a feeling you'd be back soon, so I came out to meet you," Rit admitted with a bashful expression.

Maybe it was only the cold, but her cheeks were tinged with crimson.

It had taken longer than I had expected, but apparently, Rit had foreseen exactly when I'd be back. She knew her stuff when it came to things like this.

"Hmm."

Rit looked at my face and made an expression like she noticed something.

And then she took her gloves off.

"Hey."

She put both of her hands on my cheeks. They were still warm from being in her gloves and felt great. It was as though they were gradually melting away the cold that had seeped into me.

"Your face is getting red. How is it? Warm?"

"Yeah…thank you."

Rit's hands were nice, of course, but I could feel just as much heat welling up inside of me. My heart may have started beating a bit faster, too.

"Ah!"

As I immersed myself in the comfort of Rit's tenderness, she caught my attention with a soft exclamation.

"The sky!"

"Hmm?"

Rit looked pleased about something as she looked into the air.

Turning my head upward again, I saw small white flakes fluttering down from the dark, starry night sky. I had been thinking how cold it all was, but I would never have guessed it would snow.

"This is pretty rare for Zoltan. I guess it got carried in by the winds from the Wall at the End of the World."

"It's the first time I've seen snow since coming here. I thought I'd had enough of it back in Loggervia, but seeing it like this, it looks lovely!"

"Yeah. It's not going to pile up here, either, so we can watch it fall without having to worry about dealing with it later."

Rit's homeland—the Duchy of Loggervia—was far to the north. Come winter, and it was bathed in uniform whiteness no matter where you looked. You wouldn't find piles and piles of snow like that in Zoltan, but had Rit ever been able to see it fluttering gently down like this in Loggervia?

I gently pulled her closer.

"Shall we go watch it fall for a bit?" I proposed.

"Are you sure? It's pretty cold."

"True. I don't have any heaters left, either."

I had intended to make enough to have some leftover, but the reviews were surprisingly good, and when I was at the tavern explaining the product, a bunch of nearby patrons who had never come to our shop before had gathered around.

While great for business, it had left me without any Loggervian heaters for myself. That's why I'd been so chilly when Rit found me.

"Heh-heh-heh," Rit said, breaking into a big grin. "The truth is... Ta-daa."

Rit pretentiously pulled one of the heaters out from her cleavage with a flourish.

"I thought it would be a good idea to have one to show off in case any customers happened to stop by, so I set one aside."

"Oooh, great thinking."

But now there were two of us and only one heater. The numbers didn't add up.

"I'm still okay, so you warm yourself up," Rit said as she put the pouch into my hand. "I'm from Loggervia; this level of cold is nothing special."

"No way. I couldn't bear to see you freeze while I'm comfortable."

"Nrrr."

I rejected her suggestion, of course. But I knew full well how stubborn Rit could be at times like this. At this rate, it would end with neither of us using the heater, which would be a waste, too. *Hrmph...*

After thinking about it a bit, I took Rit's hand with the heater still in my palm and started walking.

"Let's go for a little stroll."

"?"

Rit followed my lead as I pushed forward, turning off onto a path that led into the trees. Walking down the narrow route with the fallen leaves underfoot, we came to a little clearing.

"I'm sure no one will bother us here at this time of night."

"Huh? Uh? Is something going to happen? Are you going to do something?"

Rit suddenly flushed crimson and started fidgeting. She was glancing over at me as she hid her mouth behind the red bandanna around her neck.

Huh? W-wait, I didn't mean it that way...

"Ah, ummm, pardon me."

"Eh?"

I undid the buttons on my cloak and then pulled Rit close enough that it would cover both of us. The heater was right between us as we locked eyes. This way, the warmth would protect us from the cold winter night.

"This way, neither of us will freeze."

"Ah."

Rit turned the color of a beet as she hastily looked away, and then she glanced back at my face as her hands wavered before she finally wrapped them around my back and embraced me.

"...Your body is so warm," Rit said as her eyes narrowed.

Rit's cute face was right in front of me, and just a little bit of snow had gotten tangled in her pretty blond hair. I caught a whiff of a pleasant scent.

Rit's chest had gotten a bit sweaty in her coat, and I could feel it press against my own as she hugged me closer.

Rit was blushing as she looked up at me, her expression filled with pure, straightforward affection. After calming down a bit, she looked at the sky.

"Seeing it like this... The snow really is gorgeous."

Her words caused something to tingle on the back of my neck, but my eyes stayed locked on her face.

"What is it? All you've done is look at me... You see it all the time, right? What about the snow?"

"But I'll never get to see you in the snow at this moment again... I was captivated by it."

Oh no, I didn't mean to say what I was thinking out loud. What am I doing? I could feel my cheeks burning.

"S-sorry for saying such a weird thing." I frantically tried to make an excuse for myself as Rit listened in openmouthed surprise. I really thought I'd screwed up.

"Eh-heh... Eh-heh-heh..." As I started to fidget, Rit broke into a happy grin. "I'm the one who was caught off guard there, so why are you the one turning so red?" Rit's cheeks were bright scarlet, and she was grinning as she teased me in a tone that was light and playful, like she was floating on sunshine.

"I didn't mean to surprise you... I was just embarrassed because my thoughts slipped out."

"Aren't you a bashful one."

Instead of replying, I pressed my forehead against Rit's.

As the snow fell from the night sky, we held each other close beneath a single coat. Our heads were pressed together as we giggled. There were no signs of anyone else nearby.

"It's just the two of us."

Rit was thinking the same thing that I was. It made me want to laugh. It felt so lovely I couldn't stand it. I kissed her softly.

I focused all five of my senses on Rit as my heart swelled like it was about to burst.

Our lips broke apart as we shared a bashful smile and then looked at the sky.

"The snow is pretty."

"Yeah."

We were huddled together under a single jacket, warmed by a

solitary heater, watching the snow fall under the cold night sky. This kind of quiet life was excellent.

"After this, I'm sure everyone will want to come buy a heater tomorrow."

"Yeah, I imagine so."

"I'm sure sales will be much better tomorrow," Rit said as she smiled at me.

Seeing that grin suddenly made me realize why I'd wanted to do something about the lack of customers. It was because I had wanted to be able to share happy moments like this one alongside Rit.

Worrying with her, making something as a team, and then either celebrating or feeling dejected together. I just wanted the time with her.

"There's no telling whether customers will actually come tomorrow, though."

"Really? I think they will."

"Thanks. I was able to give it my all today because you believed in me."

Rit tilted her head slightly as she looked up at me. She squeezed her arms tight around me again, pulling closer. "Don't push yourself too hard. I'm happy just being able to watch the snow with you." She blushed and broke into a loose smile. I couldn't help but grin.

"Right, enjoying myself with you isn't something I have try at."

"Exactly. You've already done so much. So for my sake, try not to overreach."

In the grand scheme of things, if I could be together with Rit like this, then that was enough. Rit would stay with me regardless of what I achieved.

"It truly is warm like this."

"Yeah... It really is..."

Night fell as we stood there. Moonlight cast a pale glow on the snow that danced as it fluttered to the ground.

The two of us shared a quiet night looking at the sky.

Chapter 2
- - - - - - - - -
The Hero, Just One Step Away

By the next day, I had made preparations to head to the mountains.

Our supply of herbs was finally getting low, and we hadn't had many rust-eating mushrooms in our inventory to begin with. With winter coming, different medicines would become more critical. I was going to have to stock up on everything.

"All right, I'll be back soon."

"Take care. And here's your lunch."

Incidentally, I had made almost the entire lunch. The crunchy, over-easy egg was the only portion Rit had made. I'd wondered why she had come into the kitchen all of a sudden early in the morning. She'd said she wanted to give me my lunch when I left. Evidently, it wouldn't have felt right if she handed it to me without actually contributing some part of its contents at all. Thus, I'd had her cook me some fried eggs.

"Mfh." Rit looked satisfied as she gave me the packaged meal.

As I headed for the mountain, I saw that a knight was still standing in the middle of the bridge, blocking everyone who tried to cross. It would be annoying to deal with him, so I just took the long way around like last time.

Does he just have a lot of free time on his hands or something?

∗   ∗   ∗

Nooo, I don't want to! I practically screamed the thought.

Before me was the drainage ditch where the village's wastewater, sewage, and all sorts of other trash were dumped. In the muck, there was a wooden wyvern toy floating, caught up on some garbage.

"Waaaaaaaaaaah!"

A boy was crying as he pointed to the bauble in the ditch. He had probably dropped it.

There was a stomach-churning stench rising from the gulley, and various unknown objects had precipitated out. Each was so unpleasant that I wanted to look away.

If that kid would only have given up and left, I could have endured it. But he wouldn't quit, and he refused to stop bawling.

Maybe he knew about my peculiarity. Perhaps his crying was calculated. I didn't think that was the case, but once that seed of doubt had been planted in me, it swelled and turned into an incurable hatred that scorched my heart.

I am the Hero. I can't turn away from someone in need—even if I was younger than him. It didn't matter that I was on my way to go play somewhere. I'd done something like this before and gotten my clothes dirty. My mother had beaten me for it and had told me never to do something like this again, but that was of no consequence.

My blessing paid no heed to my personal circumstances.

I can't take it anymore. I was going to jump down, trudge through all that filth, and ruin this whole day for the sake of a toy that wasn't even worth a single bronze coin.

I started limply walking toward the drainage when someone grabbed my shoulder.

"Leave it to me."

He didn't hesitate at all to jump into the ditch. He grimaced as he walked waist-deep into the muck, marched firmly toward the toy, picked it up, and walked back.

"Here. Don't drop it again. Also, it's dirty, so go wash it off."

"Thank you, Gideon!"

The boy who had just been bawling smiled happily and ran off, clutching the soiled toy.

"Haaah..." My savior looked at the spectacle he had become and smiled bitterly.

I started to move closer, but he frantically stopped me.

"You'll get dirty."

"...Big Brother..."

My protector was my one and only big brother.

"I'm sorry."

"Why are you apologizing? You didn't do anything wrong."

"But..."

"I just did it because I wanted to. Don't worry about it."

"I understand...... Big Brother..."

"What?"

"Sorry. I can't."

I embraced him, even though my clothes would get dirty. Big Brother tried to push me away at first, but when he noticed that I was crying, he accepted it and let me hug him.

"Let's go wash our clothes."

"Okay."

A real hero was someone more like my big brother. He was the kind of person who would jump into the sewage of his own volition. I only did it because my blessing compelled me to.

I wanted to defeat the demon lord because it would save the most people in need. That way, I wouldn't be troubled by urges to perform small acts of mercy like this.

I couldn't have cared less about something like the fate of the world.

✳   ✳   ✳

Ruti and Tisse were proceeding along the road toward Zoltan.

Ruti was not wearing her usual armor, nor was the Holy Demon Slayer hanging at her waist.

When Tisse had pointed out that those would draw too much attention, the Hero had obediently put them into her item box and then disappeared off somewhere for about ten minutes.

While Tisse waited, wondering where she had gone, Ruti came back holding a sword. And for some reason, there were three goblins following behind her. They were carrying baskets woven from tree branches that had dried river fish inside.

"Uh, um, did something happen?"

"I noticed that some goblins were nearby, so I borrowed a weapon."

The sword in her hand was a two-handed weapon with three holes in the blade—a goblin blade. Tisse was worried it might snap in half as Ruti casually swung it.

"Well, if it's in a sheath, no one will know... And what about those goblins behind you?"

"The chief of their settlement had collapsed because of some illness, so I used my Healing Hands. As thanks, I got this weapon and some food."

"Huh? Ah, you don't say? ...Is it really okay to be aiding goblins?"

"It's fine. Their village wasn't involved with any pillaging. Around forty percent of all goblins survive off hunting and simple farming. They don't all go out raiding. These kinds tend to live far away from humans, though, so you don't see them often."

The Hero's strength lay not just in defeating villainy, but in recognizing what was evil, too. Tisse was filled with a newfound reverence for Ruti.

"Understood. That sword might be good for looking the part of a simple adventurer. Let's put the food away into our item boxes."

"Okay."

The Hero smiled happily after Tisse approved of her actions, but the smirk was so faint that Tisse didn't notice it.

With the goblins thanking them, the two of them turned away and left the airship.

*   *   *

Zoltan's grasslands billowed in the wind.

The northern forest where Ruti and Tisse had landed the airship already showed signs of winter, but Zoltan still seemed to be in autumn. The plains were changing color from green to brown, lending the landscape an almost forlorn sort of feeling.

"It's still quite cool despite being farther south."

"It is," Ruti responded flatly.

Because of Ruti's Environmental Resistance, cold was nothing more than a trivial bit of information. From extreme arctic frost to scorching desert heat, no temperature was capable of impeding the Hero. After walking for a little bit, the two of them caught sight of a crowd.

"What's this about? I'm going to go check it out real quick."

Tisse used her small frame to slip through the gathered mass. She quickly returned back to Ruti.

"Some knight is apparently blocking the bridge. A supposedly capable adventurer challenged him but was defeated. It would be a bit of a detour, but there is another way around. Shall we go that way?"

"No, we'll cross here." Ruti headed straight for the crowd. "Out of the way," she ordered.

"Hey, Missy, be careful. There's a weird knight barring passage over…" A man started to say something, but partway through, he realized that his legs were quivering. "Oh… Whoaaaaa…"

He instinctively yielded the path. Seeing that, the other people naturally formed a route for Ruti. It wasn't until the blue-haired girl left that they finally realized they'd been frightened of her.

On the bridge was a knight wearing armor and wielding a spear with cloth wrapped around the tip to avoid killing his opponents.

He was a large man, over six and a half feet tall.

"This is a toll. If you want to pass, then you'll need one hundred payril," the knight declared.

"Why?" Ruti asked, tilting her head.

"Why? Because I want to."

"I see. Then I don't need to pay." Ruti advanced right toward the man but didn't even move to draw her sword.

"Wha—? Who the hell are you...?" Though his opponent was an unarmed girl, the knight couldn't bring himself to attack. For some reason, he could only envision himself getting killed.

Tisse predicted that the knight would throw down his weapon and surrender before long. However...

"Uoooooooooooh!!!" The large man roared and took a big step forward, loosing a powerful thrust. "...Huh?" The knight, who was supposed to be the one attacking, made an absurd sound, not understanding what was happening.

Ruti had casually caught the high-speed spear attack with her right hand. It looked like she was gingerly holding it with a single hand. That was all it took for her to keep her opponent's lunge from hitting her.

"You're in my way," Ruti muttered softly. She lifted the knight's body by the spear. The powerfully built man floated up into the air and then went flying.

"Whoooooa?!"

Ruti cast him aside, and he plunged into the river.

"Let's go, Tisse."

"R-right."

Tisse followed after the Hero, at his wit's end wondering why Ruti had gone and defeated him in such a spectacular way when the pair were supposed to be incognito as regular travelers.

*   *   *

As I was walking, I heard some kind of groan. Thinking it was a bit suspicious, I headed toward the source of the voice.

"Ugh...so cold."

What I found was a big man shivering next to a fire. He only had undergarments on. His clothes were hung to dry on a nearby tree.

"I almost drowned and had to take off my armor in the middle of the river. That full plate armor was expensive…"

The man was murmuring to himself, teary-eyed, as he broke a stick and tossed it into the fire.

All right, I'll just pretend I didn't see anything. Swiveling around, I started to leave, but…

"Wait! You there! Wait!"

Gh, he noticed me.

The man stomped over toward me.

Sensing it would turn into something annoying, I wanted to run away, but the freezing, nearly naked man hadn't even said anything yet. Ditching him would have been a little too harsh.

"Ah, did you need something?" I asked with a polite smile, exerting my best nonverbal "This is really a nuisance, though," sort of aura.

"My name is Otto. I'm a Drake Rider and commander of the glorious Fafnir Knights' raiders."

"That so?"

Drake Rider was a top-tier blessing in the Knight tree. As the name implied, they specialized in forming a bond with a drake and had the creature carry them into combat.

Even when both were mounted, a person with Drake Rider tended to be stronger than someone with the more common blessing Wyvern Rider.

There were several reasons for that, but the main one was that those with the Drake Rider blessing had the skill Dragon-Rider Link, which allowed them to share their skills with their mount.

Drakes had their own blessings, of course, so when it gained strength from an additional one, it could overpower an enemy who would have otherwise been on a similar level.

However, that did not necessarily mean that Drake Rider was an incredible blessing. It bore a critical weakness—you could only form a bond with a single drake. All the powerful skills they had access to would be gone, never to return, if that one beast died. If that happened, the remaining skills granted by the blessing were nothing more than what the lowest tier Cavalier blessing had access to. All the points spent on skills for their partner would suddenly leave them even weaker than a similarly leveled Cavalier.

Thus…

"…And so my partner was killed by the horrid giant Grendel as I slew it."

It was used for lots of "I used to be really strong" sort of tales.

"Hmm? What? The Fafnir Knights?"

Mogrim the blacksmith mentioned a creature named Fafnir before, didn't he? Maybe the word was some new sort of trend.

"Yes, the Fafnir Knights! We may not be well-known to people living out on the frontier, but there isn't a soul in the capital who doesn't know the glorious Fafnir Knights, third only to the renowned Bahamut Knights and the ruthless Tiamat Knights! I was a Drake Rider for that resplendent faction."

"I've never heard of them."

"Well, you live in Zoltan, so it isn't surprising that you're not up on the current news in Central. It's nothing to be ashamed of," Otto said as he patted my shoulder to console me.

I glared coolly at the man.

Once upon a time, I was second in command of those Bahamut Knights you so callously mentioned.

"So what does the noble knight need of me? I was in a bit of a hurry."

"Right! I wanted to ask you a favor."

"A favor?"

"You see, the reason I've come to Zoltan is to slay the hill giant Dundach and claim its castle to become a land-owning aristocrat."

Now that was something I was familiar with.

Three years ago, five hill giants had appeared, attacking the castle of a lord who resided to the northwest of Zoltan and claimed it for themselves. Zoltan had sent out a force to exterminate them, but they were routed. The giants had already killed the nobleman, so everyone in Zoltan had been content just to let it be ever since.

Brash adventurers with dreams of owning a castle would occasionally try to take back the keep—never to return—but other than that, the giants never caused much trouble.

"Hmmm, I see. Well, good luck with that."

"Wait, wait, wait! Let me finish."

I had started to leave, but Otto frantically called me back.

"That's why, to find someone capable of fighting the giants at my side, I've been challenging the people crossing the bridge."

"Oh, so you're that troublesome knight?"

"And then, today, I was finally able to meet a woman who was my equal in strength. This must be fate! I'm going to find that warrior, and we shall defeat the evil hill giants and claim the castle!" Having made his gallant declaration, Otto flushed a bit, like he was slightly embarrassed. "And then I will propose to her, and we'll live together in the castle."

"Oh, I see. I hope it works out for you two."

"Wait, wait, wait! I'm almost done. I'm getting to the point."

Otto frantically called me back as I started to leave again.

Just get on with it already, please.

"So what is it that you want me to do?"

"It's really nothing that big, but..." He was fidgeting nervously. Seeing a six-and-a-half-foot-tall man act like that was hardly endearing.

"When I was thrown into the river, my weapons, armor, belongings, and all the money I had on me were washed away... Could you lend me some coin? I'll repay you once I have my castle."

"Not interested," I fired back immediately.

"Even if I got on my knees?"

"Yep."

"You leave me with no alternative, sir! I will use force if I must! Set all of your money on the ground!"

At that, Otto raised his hands and charged me in his underwear.

"If you don't want to be hurt, then jus— Arrgggggghhhh?!"

The next thing either of us knew, I had plowed a full-powered fist into his face.

Agh, that's no good. I just reflexively punched him. I generally made a point of not biting when someone was fishing for a fight so I wouldn't stand out, but honestly, something about him got to me on an instinctual level.

Otto flew backward, falling into the river again with a big splash. His body floated up to the surface and drifted downstream.

He was only a highwayman, so I guess that much is fine. I'd best keep moving.

*   *   *

Zoltan experienced short autumns.

I hadn't gotten a chance to enjoy the season on the mountain before the leaves fell, and it transformed into a desolate winter landscape.

"Even if the snow doesn't stick, the cold still limits the herbs you can find this time of year."

There were ones that could only be found in winter, too, like polyp mushrooms, an ingredient for medicine that treated cholera. There were also snow vines that helped with the infections one developed from open wounds. Thankfully, you could still find gray starfish grass and rust-eating mushrooms, too.

But it would hurt not being able to gather the henbane used for hemostatics and disinfectants or koku leaves for antidotes or all the other ingredients for medicines that were in high demand.

I needed to gather up as much as possible while there was still anything left to be found.

"A greenhouse sure would help to deal with seasonal plants."

I made a note to ask Gonz about it when I returned home. But for now, I needed to focus on gathering.

If you chimeras are going to keep watching me, the least you could do is help out, too.

The monsters staring at me from a distance dashed away in a panic when I glanced over at them.

*   *   *

My name is Tisse. A long time ago, I was an assassin, but now I'm just a person at my wit's end.

Naturally, the source of my troubles is the Hero.

"I'm just a traveler. I'm not suspicious at all."

Those were the exact words she'd said to the guardsmen at Zoltan's gate. She was carrying a greater giant frog that looked like it weighed a thousand pounds over her shoulder.

Why?

Not ten minutes ago, I had given one of the gatekeepers a false story while slipping him a little bribe. Everything was going just fine. All the Hero had to do was wait patiently. There should've been no issue.

"U-um, Ms. Ruhr."

Ruhr was the Hero's alias while we were in the town. Incidentally, my moniker was Tifa.

The basic story was that Ruhr was searching for her father, who had gone missing. I didn't know much about the alchemist that the Hero was actually seeking, but given that we were looking for someone, making the target of the search a family member seemed acceptable. Once we found the alchemist, we could just write it off as him as being the wrong person who just happened to resemble Ruhr's father. Yet somehow, we ended up in this compromising predicament.

"What's with that frog on your back?"

"It was hibernating in the ground nearby. I thought it would be dangerous come spring, so I exterminated it."

"Y-yeah. Well, okay, I guess. But why are you carrying it?"

"?"

"Come on, please don't just tilt your head." I groaned.

"If you defeat an animal or magical beast near a town, you turn it in at the local exchange," Ruti stated matter-of-factly.

I mean, yeah, but come on!

A guard tapped my shoulder. I turned so stiffly that I was afraid my joints were creaking audibly. When I met the man's eyes, I saw that they were practically sparkling.

"Your friend there is amazing. I'll go get a cart from the butcher, so wait here a bit."

The Hero seemed aloof, unbothered by the praise and curious gazes she was garnering from every direction.

"Ms. Ruhr, a guardsmen said he'd get a cart from the butcher. So you can set the frog down."

"Okay."

There was a resounding, rumbling thud as the massive amphibian hit the ground.

Argh, I'm sure there will be rumors about us spreading around the town now.

So much for keeping a low profile…

*   *   *

At this time of year, the nights on the mountain were cold. I shivered as I wrapped myself in a sleeping bag.

The campfire was crackling.

I slipped a heater I had made into the sleeping bag and sighed as it worked its magic.

Because the mountains were close to the Wall at the End of the World, the wind was freezing. The gales that came from the north were especially biting.

"I miss my bed."

In the past, I'd never felt particularly attached to my house. Truth be told, I'd even considered erecting a little lodge up here. Being able to stay in the wilds for two or three nights would have significantly increased my spoils. However, those plans had been shelved.

I wanted to spend as much time back at the house as possible.

"Hmm, I guess this is what it means to have a 'home.'"

I fell asleep amid thoughts of Rit waiting for me.

The next day, I gathered all that I could, and when it started getting dark, I headed down the mountain.

While no one is watching, I should use Lightning Speed to get back to Zoltan as soon as possible.

Eagerly, I sprinted full speed back toward town.

"Heeeey!" I shouted, waving down the guard who was about to close the gate.

"Oh, is that Red I see? Back from gathering medicinal herbs?"

"Yeah. Can you let me in?"

"Too much work. Just climb over the wall there."

"I don't want to. That's too much work for me."

We bantered a bit as the guard waited a little longer to finish shutting the barricade. Zoltan's ramparts were little more than a stone wall that barely rose beyond six feet. If you wanted to, it wasn't that hard to climb over.

Adventurers who were too late and missed the gate closing for the night just hopped the wall, but there was an unspoken agreement that everyone turned a blind eye to the practice.

People sneaking in after dark would have been a big problem anywhere else, but in Zoltan, folks were laid-back enough to laugh it off.

"You sure are good at coming in just at the last moment."

"That's because I take the rules seriously."

"If that's true, then how about getting back before the eleventh hour next time! Anyway, I'm heading out now. How about a drink?"

"Thanks, but no. I'm going home."

"Where's the love? Choosing your girlfriend over me?"

"Damn straight."

"You don't have to be so blunt about it… Fine. How about just the one drink?"

"Weeell, it has been a long time since we went out for a mug. Sure, I guess. I'll stick around to down one with you at the food stall."

Spending time with friends was important, too, but I had no intention of staying out late.

We left the gate and went to a mobile *oden* stand along the border between the harbor district and the working-class neighborhood.

"Welcome."

Usually, a gruff, unmarried old man greeted you when you approached the cart. Today, however, it was a platinum-blond, slender, well-proportioned, and stylish high elf woman.

The shop's owner was getting up there in years. When he'd mentioned retirement, the high elf Oparara had said, "I can't bear to see this place close, so if you're going to quit, then let me succeed you!"

That old dog was a sucker when it came to beautiful women, so after standing his ground for about thirty seconds, he gave in to Oparara, and the two of them had started pulling the stall together. Lately, Oparara was running it on her own more often.

Seeing her reminded me of my old comrade, Yarandrala, though there was no comparison when it came to bust size.

High elves ruled the Kingdom of Kiramin, making them the only other race besides humans to wear one of Avalon's official crowns.

The dwarf king who lived on Sir Beard Mountain only bore the official title of duke, and Sir Beard Mountain was just a self-ruled territory, not a kingdom.

Unlike the colloquial phrase for a hereditary ruler, a proper king or queen only referred to one of the officially recognized kingdoms' monarchs. On Avalon, those territories all belonged to either humans or high elves.

That was why high elves professed themselves to be noble creatures. Humans, perhaps not wishing to think on it too deeply, had no problems acquiescing to that declaration. However, half-elves, who were the descendants of the wood elves who once dominated the continent, and the wild elves, who had stepped away from civilization but were nonetheless directly descended from the ancient elves, regarded their haughty cousins as merely urban things—city elves.

As for me, well, I just called them high elves. I mean, I'm human, too, and calling them urban elves was an excellent way to piss them off.

Fundamentally, high elves tended to be quite open about what they thought and felt, always speaking their mind. If they got upset, they would not hesitate to insist that they had been hurt by what you had said. In one sense, that made them difficult to get along with, but in another, it made them easy to get to know.

Of course, each high elf had their quirks. There were plenty of them who could talk out of both sides of their mouth, too. They weren't incapable of putting up a front. It was just that, as a rule, high elves generally didn't like doing so, and thus they didn't bother. If they put their mind to it, they were capable of being far more devious than humans. In particular, the captain always used to say that you could never trust the Kiramin royalty.

On that point, Yarandrala was straightforward and agreeable. As I recalled my time with her, I wondered if she was still traveling together with Ruti and the others. The journey was undoubtedly rough, but I hoped she was doing well, regardless.

"I'll have daikon and beef tendon, egg, and *hanpen*. And a beer, please," the guard said as he pointed to various things floating in the square pot.

"And I'll take daikon, a wiener, and some *chikuwa*, too. And a cup of beer."

"Gotcha!" Oparara responded with a forceful, high elf voice that sounded like a bell chime.

She fished our orders into a pair of wooden bowls with a practiced motion.

"That reminds me..."

Oparara glanced at the bag of herbs on the ground as she passed me my meal.

"Are you not selling mustard seeds anymore, Boss?"

Oparara used to call me Red before she opened the stall. Apparently, she'd even started adopting the cart's previous owner's speech patterns. High elves sure were meticulous.

"Ah, I don't go into the mountains as often as I used to. Any spices I gather, I use myself," I replied.

"That's too bad. I'm going to have to find a steady source in town, then."

The going price for mustard seeds was five payril per kilogram at the trading post. And it got higher once it went to market. The spice went well with *oden*, but it wasn't free. That was why the guard and I hadn't asked for it.

A lone girl appeared at the counter.

"Welcome!"

"Daikon, beef tendon, egg, and four *chikuwa*. And mustard."

"Gotcha!"

Taking the bowl from Oparara, the girl didn't hesitate to add in all the mustard provided on a small plate at the side.

That style, that regal way of eating *oden*! It was so carefree. It practically screamed "I'll just ask for more if I run low!"

Amazing!

Four *chikuwa* was its own sort of unusual, too. I guess she just really liked them.

Anyway, she was a new face. Short, but her body had clearly been well trained. Her black hooded outfit had been worn down some from travel, but it was high quality.

There was a shortsword at her waist. Inside the cloak, she had three throwing knives strapped beneath her armpit. The shortsword had a magical enhancement and some other kind of special effect applied to it. It also bore some concealing magic to hide all of that. There was mithril chainmail woven into the underside of her garment.

Her gear emphasized practicality, and it had been designed to appear like everyday items to avoid standing out.

She's a strong one. Maybe an adventurer who's been wandering for a while… Seems like she's trying to keep aloof. Probably some kind of job where she needs to be careful not to be noticed. A thief or a spy…or else maybe an assassin?

At that moment, the girl suddenly glanced over at me.

"Yes?" she asked expectantly.

"Ah, sorry. I was just curious since I hadn't seen you around before.

And it looks like you're doing well enough for yourself to order the mustard, too."

"Mustard is a must for *oden*."

"I hope I can make enough to be able to say that, too, someday."

It had only been a sidelong glance, but she'd noticed I was looking her over. *She's pretty good. Who is she?*

At that moment:

"Ah, you're the one from yesterday!" the guard exclaimed after eyeing the girl for a moment.

"What, do you know her?" I asked.

"You wouldn't believe it, Red! The girl she was with dragged this fat frog hibernating in the mud near the gate out of the ground with just one hand and used some crazy martial art I had never seen before to kill it with this beaten-up old goblin blade!"

The girl's cheek twitched. Apparently, this was a topic she would rather not discuss. Her expression was too subtle for the guardsmen to notice, however.

"What was your friend's name again? Ru...Rurt?"

"Her name is Ruhr."

I thought she would just ignore the gatekeeper, but apparently, having her comrade's name mistaken bothered her because she made a point of correcting him.

"Yeah, yeah, Ruhr! And if I remember right, your name was Tifa? If you two are planning to stick around Zoltan for a while, you should definitely go by the Adventurers Guild. There are never enough skilled quest takers around here. There are extermination jobs posted for other beasties like that fat toad that'll become trouble in the spring, but no one's taken any of them."

A greater giant frog could be a surprisingly dangerous monster, despite how it looked. It used its tongue as a weapon to catch its enemies and eat them. Though possessed of slippery skin, its teeth were like razors that could easily chew through chainmail. Even if the creature found something it couldn't gnaw through, it had the problematic habit of just swallowing whatever it caught whole.

D-rank adventurers weren't up to that sort of challenge, and even C-rank adventurers couldn't risk letting their guards down, even if they attacked in a party.

If this Ruhr character had defeated a greater giant frog by herself, then she had to be a high-level C ranker at the very least—possibly even a B ranker.

The girl named Tifa glanced at the guard as he rambled on.

"Hey, let's leave it at that. I'm sure we're bothering her," I interjected.

"Eh, really?"

"Yeah, she came here to eat *oden* in peace."

Tifa nodded in response.

The guard rubbed the back of his head apologetically.

"My bad, I got a little carried away."

"It's fine. Pardon me, I'd like to take the rest of this to go. Could I get it packed up?"

Tifa stood up with that, ordered an extra *chikuwa* and a konjac to go with what she had left, and then walked away.

"See, you ruined the mood for her," I chided as I finished off the beer left in my cup. "Anyway, I'm headed back now."

"Aw, come on, go one more round with me. I feel bad about bothering her, so comfort me a bit."

"Don't wanna."

"Gh. Oparara! Can I get a *chikuwa*, too?"

"Yeah, can I get *chikuwa*, daikon, and some chicken to go, please? I'm going to take some back for Rit."

I put a quarter payril and a few commons on the counter to cover my bill.

✳   ✳   ✳

Tisse returned to her lodge in the harbor district after several roundabout detours while ensuring she wasn't being followed.

"What is it?" Ruti asked, noticing Tisse's caution.

"Please be careful. There seems to be a troublesome person here in Zoltan."

"A troublesome person?"

"He's a young man. It was just a brief encounter, but he noticed my clothes and knives," Tisse explained as she pointed to the garments interwoven with mithril chainmail and the knives hidden beneath them.

Tisse's equipment had been designed not to make a sound louder than a pin drop no matter how violently she moved. She was quite sure that an average person, or even someone with the Investigator or Detective blessing, would not be able to spot them readily.

"Not only did he see through that, but he is also quite powerful. Most likely, he has a level similar to mine. If I was forced to fight him on his terms, I doubt I would win. Obviously, that wouldn't apply to you, however."

Even if Tisse paled in comparison to the Hero, she had been chosen by Ares and was one of the best in the Assassins Guild. She was not going to feign modesty about her strength. It was a simple fact that she was skilled. And with that assessment of herself, she could also say that that man at the *oden* stand could end up being one of the highest-tier opponents she had ever encountered.

"There is no way someone that powerful would be living in obscurity. He's undoubtedly the strongest adventurer in Zoltan," Tisse decided.

"The story at the tavern was that the strongest person in Zoltan right now was a B-rank adventurer named Bui," Ruti replied.

"As far as the public is concerned, I'm sure. The way he carried himself had a certain elegance to it. If I had to guess, I'd say he learned proper etiquette in some knight order."

"A knight order..."

The face of a very familiar person flashed through Ruti's mind.

There were many knights in the world, though. That guy on the bridge she couldn't really remember anymore had called himself a knight, too. Ruti curbed the rising tide of her thoughts there.

Tisse continued without noticing any of that.

"A former knight—and probably a valiant warrior who fought on the front lines against the demon lord's armies throughout a storied career. Maybe he suffered some dishonor and drifted out to the frontier. Adventurers wouldn't pay much heed to a little bit of dirt, but as a knight, it causes problems for the entire order."

"I see."

"I can't say for sure what it would have been, but…" Tisse paused in thought for a moment. "This is just a guess, but being so young and skilled, his superior officer may have held a grudge, and he forced him into a duel where he slew the officer. Maybe something like that. I can't imagine someone that skilled merely running away after some sort of lesser failure."

"I see."

Tisse removed her sword belt. Sitting down on a bed, she heaved a sigh.

"I had thought it was strange. There aren't any proper adventurers in Zoltan. The strongest is only B rank. So how did they manage to drive an upper-tier demon away?"

It wasn't much, but Tisse had at least heard a bit of what had happened in Zoltan when Ares was interrogating Albert.

An upper-tier demon and a B-rank adventurer had conspired together and had been defeated by some skilled mystery man. However, according to what Tisse and Ruti heard in Zoltan, the guards and a wandering adventurer had resolved things together. That adventurer was currently registered as a B ranker.

"That was the story told to the public. The gallant who stopped it was surely that man at the *oden* cart. And if that's the case, then he must have been with that guard to gather information about anyone who visited Zoltan. And the reason he got up so soon after I did was that I put him on edge. The fact that he was drinking from a cup instead of a mug must have been out of habitual caution to always move freely without impairment. The sort of person who always maintains battle readiness, has no interest in fame, and considers his achievements reward enough in themselves."

Tisse reflected on her inadequacy and how she had been worrying about the amount of trouble she would have covering for the Hero on this excursion. The Hero's journey was never going to be easy. Even if they were in Zoltan, enormous barriers would always stand in Ruti's path.

"We are going to have to set our plan of action."

"Plan of action?"

"Whether we cooperate with that man or face off against him. I suspect that, as a knight, his thoughts will tend to follow a similar line as yours."

"That might be difficult. The alchemist I'm searching for is apparently in the infirmary in the local prison."

"They're in jail?"

Ruti had seemingly gathered some information herself.

Tisse was a little worried that maybe she had caused some uproar or something, but the fact that no one had raised a fuss about it so far meant that probably nothing had happened. And it was not like the Hero hadn't ever done digging before.

However, her style of gathering information was to tap someone on a shoulder and ask, more menacing than a give-and-take…

Ruti had learned from the contract demon that the alchemist who had produced the medicine was a close associate of Bighawk. However, after she had taken Devil's Blessing, the contract demon stopped talking. In the end, she had not been able to learn any identifying qualities about the person she sought…

But all of Bighawk's closest associates had been thrown in prison. A person who fit the bill of being an alchemist was currently in the jail's infirmary after being cut in the shoulder during an incident.

"Given that I'm hiding the fact that I'm the Hero, it will be impossible for us to negotiate the release of the alchemist into our custody."

"That's true… Which means a prison break?"

"Yes."

"That would require taking an antagonistic stance toward the town—and toward that man as well."

"Should I meet with him directly?"

To Tisse, Ruti's question had the added implication of "Meet and defeat."

"…There is no way that you would lose, of course. That goes without saying. But I imagine he has also considered the possibility that he might be bested. An encounter without knowing what he's got up his sleeve seems unwise."

"I see."

The Hero nodded as she tilted her head slightly.

It would be hard to blame Tisse for her surplus of caution. With all the ambitious people and schemers she had encountered as an assassin, there was no way she could imagine that the man in question was just aiming to enjoy a relaxed, easygoing, slow life.

The two young women discussed their plans going forward deep into the night until the sun started to rise.

Meanwhile, Mister Crawly Wawly had curled up and was sleeping in Tisse's bag.

The next day.

Ruti was gathering information around Zoltan again.

What we need is…

As she walked along a street in the northern district, the phantom of a man appeared in Ruti's mind and started walking alongside her.

"Okay, all we really need to know is the room where that alchemist is being held. Still, there's no guaranteeing someone knowledgeable about the prison layout is just conveniently hanging around. Inquiring about such a topic would definitely draw suspicion. We don't know this town well, and we don't have any connections. There's nothing to do but investigate on-site."

"You're right. We don't have enough time to check in a more round-about way, so let's take the usual approach."

The man was a young but battle-tested warrior.

He had been a member of the Kingdom of Avalonia's elite Bahamut order of knights before even reaching the age of ten, a hero who could list dozens of accomplishments domestically and on foreign soil—Gideon Ragnason.

Ruti's swordsmanship and her knowledge of traveling had all been taught to her by her older brother, Gideon. He had kindly, but without any compromise, taught her everything from the fundamentals of gathering information to developing the knack for recognizing what intelligence was true and what wasn't, to the tactics needed to fight a pitched battle in the field or siege a fortress, and countless other things.

Even now, while Ruti was far more powerful than Gideon, Ruti's entire line of inquiry started with the question of what her brother would do in her situation.

"What we need is the jail's daily itinerary. That and the location of the prison's infirmary. If possible, a general count of how many staff work in the sickroom would be nice, too."

"Agreed. I'll try listening from near the prison until the evening."

"Good thinking. With your perception, you should be able to tell the location and movements of the people inside from their footsteps."

Gideon smiled…and then disappeared.

He was just a shadow created by Ruti's mind.

He had only grinned because Ruti had wished for it… It was an empty expression. Ruti could feel her heart aching. The emotions that the Hero's blessing had suppressed were gradually starting to push against the container trapping them in her heart.

I miss him.

Ruti wanted to see him and talk about so much. She could convey a lot more now than before. She would not be left standing there sad and alone, unable to do anything as her big brother departed.

*No, I **will** meet him.*

The Hero's resolve warped the air around her, sending birds and stray cats fleeing in terror.

It was fortunate that there weren't any people around.

*   *   *

The workshop at Red & Rit's Apothecary.

The morning rush of customers had tapered off a bit, and I was grinding down medicinal herbs with a mortar.

Lately, rumor had it that a cold had been spreading in some of the settlements and villages near Zoltan. As a result, I had been getting orders for medicine from traveling merchants and had been able to sell out my entire stock at once.

That also meant that many people were suffering from sickness, so I couldn't get that excited about it.

All I could do was continue to prepare more remedies to get into the hands of those who needed them as soon as possible.

"Red."

Hearing my name, I stopped my work and turned around. Rit was standing there with her red bandanna around her neck, holding four leather bladders in her hands.

"What's all that?" I asked.

Standing up, I took two of the bags from her. Shaking them a bit, I could hear the slosh of a liquid.

"Liquor?"

"Yep!" a shrill voice responded. A small, winged figure appeared from behind Rit. "It's strong red wine!"

"A fairy dragon?"

Its scales had a fundamental green tone, but the way they reflected the light that came in through the windows gave them a rainbow shimmer. The tongue flickering out of the creature's mouth was a bright flaming red. It had sharp claws at the end of its four limbs, and its tail was swaying gently.

While it looked like a typical dragon, its wings were closer to a butterfly's, and it was the size of a kitten.

The fairy dragon fitfully flittered around me.

"Hello!"

"Hello. I'm Red."

"I know! I'm Kurukururu."

"I see. Nice to meet you Kurukururu."

Fairy dragons looked like dragons, but they were actually a type of fay.

I hadn't spoken with any like this since coming to Zoltan, but when I was traveling with Ruti, there were times when we went to fairy settlements looking for magic items or help solving issues for villages troubled by some fay prank.

It had been rough, but compared to the bloody incidents caused by the demon lord's army or various monsters, dealing with fay creatures could be rather charming. I could still remember bursting out laughing when some sprites had poured a bucket of water over Danan's head as a joke.

"So then, what is it?"

"Ummm, could you please help us?"

"Apparently, a disease of unknown origin is spreading through a fay settlement," Rit elaborated.

Ahhh, so the wineskins are to pay for diagnosis and medicine, then. Fay liquor was rare, and you could trade it for prices.

"I don't know how much I'll be able to help, but let me see those afflicted."

The fairy dragon let out a cute little roar.

$$* \qquad * \qquad *$$

Rit used her magic to summon a spirit dire wolf that we rode. It took us about four hours.

We left the road far behind, going deep into a muddy wetland region and through meadows that had seemingly never been touched by humans before, arriving at a fay village located at a lake with sacred lotuses floating all around.

"Welcome! Welcome!" the fairy dragon riding on my head shouted in a cheerful, shrill voice.

Drawn by its voice, several tiny little figures flew out from behind a fallen tree.

"Kurukururu is back!"

"I'm here! I brought Red!"

"Yaaaay!"

It wasn't just fairy dragons, either. There were pixies with pale, translucent wings and fifty-centimeter-tall brownies with large heads. Curiously, all the little beings seemed to know me already.

I couldn't remember interacting with any fay since coming to Zoltan.

"So this is what a fay village is like. Look over there, Red—that big mushroom has a window! They stretched a droplet of water to be like glass!" Rit certainly appeared amused as she took in the sights around the tiny village.

"Were there not any fay villages in Loggervia?"

"I've heard stories about there being some, but normally you'd never get invited into one. I did meet a brownie that lived in an old house once, though." Rit's Spirit Scout blessing granted her the power to control spirit magic, so she naturally fit in well with fairies and their ilk, since so many of them used spirit magic, too.

I knew from the past that fays hated large mountain ranges like the Wall at the End of the World for some reason, so I would have thought you wouldn't find them in Zoltan, but they had built this settlement reasonably close by.

"We hate that mountain! That's why we're on the other side of the river!" a nearby pixie explained when I asked.

Apparently, it was safe as long as they had a river between them and the mountains. Maybe there was some magical significance behind it.

I would have liked to ponder that a little longer, but that wasn't why we were here today. Shaking my head, I turned my attention back to the job at hand. "All right, shall we get to work?"

Flittering sprites and fairy dragons guided us to the fallen tree. Ducking through the small door in the timber, we entered and saw that the inside was the size of a normal house—maybe some fay spell.

"What is this? It's so cute."

Rit was looking at a small, round, alabaster, seemingly child-size teapot. As she stared, the object transformed from a glossy white to red.

"Huh?"

Rit was taken aback by the change as the pot twisted its porcelain body and started to spew a white steam from its mouth, seemingly embarrassed by the attention.

A pixie flew around Rit, laughing cheerfully before grabbing the pot by the handle with both hands while another fairy brought a small cup and poured some piping-hot tea.

"Here you go!"

"Th-thank you."

The fay creatures were frolicking around, enjoying Rit's reactions. It was a delightful scene, but I nudged Rit to continue into the next room.

"Sorry. But wow, fay villages sure are amazing."

"They're behaving themselves because they know we're here to cure some of their sick, but normally, there would be no end to their pranks."

"At least it'd keep things from getting boring."

"You can't really get in without an invitation, though."

Ares could probably force his way in using his magic, but doing that would mean dealing with the sort of serious prank that the fays reserved to drive out unwanted guests.

"Over here!"

The fairy dragon that had guided us this far waved its tiny arms while floating in front of the door to the next room. That must have been where the afflicted were resting.

Rit and I headed through the doorway and into a chamber designed for human use. There was a cute, rounded wardrobe and an ordinary wooden table and chairs. But in the stand on the wall was a bottle with shimmering sunlight insects instead of a candle.

"I brought Red," the fairy dragon exclaimed in its shrill voice as it flew to the bed next to a window.

There were six pixies and one shimmering, beautiful maiden lying there.

"Now, this is a surprise."

The woman was an undine—a member of the four clans of archfay, one of water.

As the name suggested, archfay were powerful fay. Typically, undine were found in secret, secluded areas. I hadn't known they could live in places so close to human settlements.

"Welcome to my humble little pond. It is a pleasure to have you, Red. And you as well, Rit."

The undine listlessly raised her upper body from the bed. The blanket slipped down, revealing her almost-translucent skin and the beautiful curves of her breasts as they quivered ever so slightly.

According to legend, there was once an artist who journeyed far and wide in search of an undine. Upon finally meeting one at the end of his long adventure, he went blind at the sight of such beauty.

The figure of the archfay before me was almost like a work of art in its extreme elegance, so I could understand how a story like that had come to be.

Wait, she's not wearing clothes? Well, fay were generally split on that. Some had the habit of covering themselves, while others didn't. For example, a pixie in the room was naked, but the brownie next to them was wearing some garment made of cloth.

"Red!"

There was a slightly angry voice from behind me as Rit's hands suddenly covered my eyes.

"Please put some clothes on, Undine!"

"Oops, I'm sorry about that."

With my vision blacked out, I could hear the water creature sounding apologetic, though there was also a trace of a childlike thrill in her voice. Even if she was "arch," she was still a fay—and thus prone to teasing and trickery.

"Sheeesh!"

Rit was still annoyed. I could feel her chest press against my back.

"Rit, it's true that Undine is beautiful, but if I had to describe it, it's more of an artistic sort of allure. I might feel moved, but nothing more. I love you, and what I feel for you is far more than that. So I'm not quite sure how to put this, but— Ummm, feeling you like that on my back is making me lose my composure, so could you please let me go?"

"Really? …Fine…" Rit was still a little bit miffed, but that at least got her willing to release me.

The watery being clad herself in a thin garment she had conjured up with magic.

"Good grief." I awkwardly smiled as I saw Rit looking sullen.

Still, Rit getting jealous was sort of cute, and I blushed just a little bit.

"With the presence of an archfay of water, it all makes sense. You were watching me even when I was by myself," I deduced. She was the one who had called for me by name.

The undine nodded.

"However, saying I was watching you is not exactly right. Sensing all the movements an expert of your level made is difficult even for me. All I saw were the memories of the water that saw you. But even that was enough to prove that you are not a normal being."

"I guess there is at least some benefit to having a high blessing level, even if that's *all* I've got." I rubbed the back of my head, feeling a bit embarrassed. I would never have guessed there would come a day when an undine praised me. I had intended to be on guard against various detection skills, but even then, I hadn't considered that the water itself might've been watching, too.

"All right. Shall I start the examination?"

Pulling myself back to the task at hand, I turned to the undine and the pixies.

"So what sort of symptoms have you been having?"

"Look at this."

At my question, the undine suddenly moved her face so close to mine that our lips were almost touching. Unlike Rit's sky-blue eyes, the archfay's were an aqua shade, one that invited you into their depths.

"Wha—?!" Rit exploded indignantly behind me.

Haaah… This fay is having fun messing with us…

Her goal wasn't merely to vex us, though, as I quickly realized there was something off about the undine.

"It's faint, but there are bags under your eyes."

"Exactly! It's unthinkable for my face to become muddied like this!" the undine exclaimed as she furrowed her brow sadly.

"Bags?" Rit tilted her head a bit at our back-and-forth. "Fay can get those?"

"They have blood flowing inside them, too, just like humans, elves, and most monsters. But their life force is much stronger than humans', so the poor circulation that would lead to bags under the eyes shouldn't happen. Normally, at least," I detailed.

This suggested something highly abnormal.

"Have you been experiencing anything unusual?" I asked.

"I feel terribly heavy. Like my body has become mud."

"It's so hard to fly."

"Too tired to play pranks."

"Flower nectar doesn't taste good."

Their symptoms almost sounded like exhaustion. Going for weeks without sleep or rest would be tiring, even for sprites and fairy dragons. However, so long as there wasn't some outside influence, they weren't the sort of creatures that'd push themselves to that point. I decided to check, to be sure, but they said they had just been playing around as they always did, and there was nothing that came to mind for them.

I concentrated and activated a skill from my blessing.

"I see."

First Aid mastery: On-the-Spot Diagnosis. It was a skill that allowed the user to discover how to ease a sick or injured person's symptoms, even without knowing the root of the problem.

"...A medicine for soothing the heart. It seems like a remedy that heals spiritual damage would be good here."

"Magics like Mind Pain and Forget can cause spiritual damage, but it's quite rare for a disease to be the source."

On-the-Spot Diagnosis was generally a skill for buying time until someone with a blessing with access to an advanced inherent skill arrived, but knowing what treatment lessened the syndrome's effects was still valuable information as a general reference.

"Did everyone start experiencing their symptoms at the same time?"

"Yes."

"By chance, do the fays here that are feeling unwell have a higher level than the others?"

"Yes, that's right! How did you know?"

So that's what it is.

"It was odd that you, who are surely the strongest fay here, would start showing signs straightaway. If an undine and pixies, all higher fay, are affected, why are none of the weaker brownies or fairy dragons suffering? It's unnatural. Whatever the illness, it wouldn't make sense for the strongest ones to be the first to collapse."

Rit nodded along with my explanation.

"Which means that this isn't an illness that spreads through infection. It's likely a sort of magic—probably a curse—that targets beings with more strength."

"A curse?"

"I suspect this is a hex that absorbs spiritual energy. What you are experiencing are the symptoms of your energy being absorbed faster than you can recover."

The undine asked the fairy dragon at her side to bring a cup of water. When she touched her fingertip to the liquid's surface, it splashed all around. The droplets started sizzling as they turned into steam.

Undoubtedly, it was some fay tactic for detecting curses.

"When did such a powerful curse...? I never noticed it."

"It must be quite potent to go unnoticed for so long. I wonder who could have cast it," I remarked.

Even with medicine to heal the spiritual damage, real recovery was impossible as long as the hex remained. The only answers I could think of off the top of my head were removing whatever the source of the curse was or erecting a barrier to block it out. Unfortunately...

"Sorry, but I don't have the ability to trace back the source of the hex, nor do I have the power to erect a barrier capable of protecting you from such a mighty curse."

"Me neither. I can use several barrier spells, but I only have access to spirit magic. I'm sure you fay possess more impressive spells than I do." Rit was a warrior worthy of being called a hero, but curses were not really her area of expertise. My old comrade Theodora, with her Blessing of the Crusader, would have been perfect. Ruti's Healing Hands would work, too.

"Is there anything you can do with your powers, Undine?"

"Even at my best, I don't believe I'd be able to handle this affliction, but I'm hardly at full strength at the moment."

"So there's someone in Zoltan more powerful than an archfay." There was a sense of excitement in Rit's voice as if her blessing was throbbing. However, she quickly reverted to a calm expression, shaking her head to brush away the impulse.

"The destruction of some powerful hex isn't a job for an apothecary," I stated bluntly.

"I see..." The undine looked despondent.

"However, there is a medicine that can nullify the effects of the curse."

Apparently, archfay were capable of going wide-eyed in surprise. The undine's statuesque, otherworldly face blossomed in joy, just like a young girl's might have.

"This curse possesses effects similar to the spell Nightmare. That being the case, there is a medicine you can take that disperses dreams.

If you imbibe it, you should be able to prevent your spiritual energy from being absorbed."

It was difficult to make a medicine that could remove a hex without having a high level in a blessing that specialized in them, like Witch or Shaman. I knew of a remedy that could dispel the curse, but it could not be made with just the common skill Elementary Preparation.

However, just like it was possible to nullify an illness's symptoms with medicine, even without removing the underlying pathogen causing the disease, it was also possible to negate the effects of a potent curse without doing anything about the source magic itself.

However, there was little research into such things since the vast majority of blessings dealing with hexes tended to have impulses toward secrecy. That had made my own research into curses rather difficult. If I hadn't been able to use my authority as a knight to get access to the city library and the lord's personal collection, I would've been as much in the dark on the subject as anyone else.

"Curses that disable their target are fairly common. If you take this medicine, you should be able to prevent your mental strength from being stolen."

"Really?!"

"Yes, you can try it out starting tonight. I currently have three days' worth of this stuff. Fortunately, the pixies should get by with a fairly small dose. I'll prepare some more when I get back to my shop, so come again tomorrow to pick it up," I instructed.

After producing the curative, I retrieved a set of scales from my item box and divided the powder into portions for each of those suffering under the curse.

"This is the dream dispersal medicine, and this is the spirit healing one. The former is best taken about one hour before going to bed, but I guess fay don't really decide when to go to sleep like that? It should be fine if you take it right before you lie down for the night. You should only need to take the spirit-healing medicine now. So long as the curse isn't getting in the way, you should all heal naturally. This one dose will just be for easing the symptoms you're already experiencing."

"Is it bitter?" a pixie sitting on the edge of a small bed asked, looking worried.

"Yeah, it's a little bit bitter."

"Don't wanna."

"But if you don't, you'll keep feeling bad like you do now."

"I don't want that, either! I guess bitter is okay!"

Hearing that it would help them feel better, the pixies started getting excited. They hadn't even taken the remedy yet, but it already seemed like they were improving.

"Whoever cast the curse probably has a powerful blessing, but I suspect they probably aren't a curse specialist. Maybe they used a magic item. We should let the Adventurers Guild know that there could be someone like that lurking in Zoltan."

Bui should be able to do something about this, right? I didn't know much about him, but from what I'd gathered during the Bighawk incident, he seemed to have the sort of real strength that was the exception out here in Zoltan.

"Yeah, the current Adventurers Guild should be able to do something about it," Rit agreed with a nod.

She knew more about Bui than I did. From how she was acting, she appeared to believe he could handle himself against an opponent more powerful than an archfay.

Hmm. I wasn't really one to talk, but why had such a skilled person come to Zoltan? My train of thought suddenly came to an end as I felt the refreshing feeling of a clear, cool, spring stream envelop my body.

"Thank you, Red!"

Snapping back to my surroundings, I saw that the undine had leaped out of bed and was clinging on to me.

"I was so worried! If you hadn't been able to help us, I'm sure we would have shriveled up like a dried-out lake!"

This time it seemed like she wasn't playing around. It was just pure-and-simple gratitude. And because Rit understood that, she didn't say anything, though she was still clearly bothered by it. As politely as I could, I peeled Undine away from me as she kissed my cheek.

She seemed to have calmed down a bit as she smiled sheepishly.

*   *   *

"Feel free to come by to play anytime. And we would gladly welcome you if you wanted to move out here."

"Come live with us!"

"Home is where you lay your head!"

"We can play every day."

The fay were flying circles all around Rit and me as they thanked us and entreated us with impassioned invitations.

"We appreciate the sentiment, but we'll have to decline. Our home is in Zoltan."

"Rejected. Whatever shall I do."

Feeling better, Undine flashed a cheeky little grin as Rit and I departed.

Rit summoned her spirit dire wolf again, and we rode toward a village up the river instead of heading straight back to Zoltan.

"The symptoms of that cold seem similar to the curse affecting the fay," Rit observed. Although practically retired from questing now, Rit still had her network of information and connections from when she was an adventurer, so she generally had a solid grasp on whatever was going on in Zoltan.

If her guess was right, then standard cold medicine would be worthless. One of the particularly nasty things about this curse was that it gradually weakened you, so someone who didn't know any better would think they were just a little under the weather at first.

There were undoubtedly those in Zoltan who could recognize it was a hex, but there was no way they would go all the way out to a distant village to do an examination. I was relieved that I'd prepared medicine that could help before things got truly urgent.

"Still, to think the day would come when I would get to visit a fay village," Rit said with wonder.

"It looked like the pixies took a liking to you," I replied.

"But that undine was awful! She was having fun seeing me get like… like that!"

"Jealous?"

Instead of answering, Rit pinched my thigh.

"Ow!"

"Sheesh! It's not like I don't know… I know that you wouldn't betray me. But I get hotheaded sometimes. So…even if I know that, my heart still starts racing." Rit seemed both upset and a little bit down. "I want to be a little more composed, since we're both in love, but…"

As Rit's shoulders slumped a bit, I gave her a big hug from behind. "I know how you are. You were really cute back in the bewitching woods with Yarandrala, too."

"Geh?!"

Rit shuddered as she gave off a strangled shout. Her ears peeking out from her blond hair were turning red as she recalled the embarrassing memory.

I had meant what I said. I could remember the lousy mood Rit had been in for a while back when we had reunited with Yarandrala in Loggervia. While we were in the woods, she'd gotten fired up with jealousy over Yarandrala. Unable to handle her feelings, her tone had gotten pretty scathing…but the affection that underpinned it had been appealing and not at all unpleasant.

Not that I had my own emotions in order back then, either, so I didn't know what that pleasant sensation I experienced around Rit was, but…well, I was younger then.

"I love you, though, including that side of you."

"Nrgh?!"

The giant wolf slowed its sprint and glanced up at me. Perhaps it had noticed Rit's agitation. I lightly patted the beast's back to reassure it. It snorted, almost as if it was shaking its head at us, before picking up speed again.

"…Really? You don't think I'm a pain to deal with?"

"I love you. Both the way you were back then and the way you are now."

"...Okay..." Rit glanced down for a moment before suddenly jerking her head up and staring at me. "I—I guess if you're going to say that much, then I'll forgive the stuff with the undine this time! Be grateful!" Flushing scarlet, Rit tried to hide the grin spreading across her face by burying her head in my chest. "I shouldn't have said that," she muttered after a moment.

"Why? You're so cute like this."

"Argh."

It would take another hour for the wolf to reach the village we were headed toward—more than enough time for the two of us to start functioning correctly again. Thankfully, that allowed Rit and me to act clumsily for a little bit longer.

"Hey, could you say it one more time?"

"No way," Rit said as she shook her head violently against my chest.

That, in its own way, was adorable, too.

After checking on the sick people in the village, I determined that the curse was the cause there, too. After that, we gave out medicine in the town and then reported the incident to the Adventurers Guild back in Zoltan.

At first, the guild seemed on the fence about whether to believe it, but since Rit was the one who reported it, they would have to believe it. Bui or some other adventurers would take care of dealing with whoever had cast the hex. If the whole point of the attack had been to absorb spiritual energy, then the caster might have given up after a medicine started to deny them that.

As an apothecary, I did my part and started making more of the remedy once the sun began setting and then turned it over to the relevant Zoltan authorities. Other doctors and apothecaries also seemed to be responding, so it should be fine. My job was done.

Today had been a good day for sales. And there was the fairy wine on top, blowing the record for daily profit away just days after Rit and I had set it.

There was a nice sense of accomplishment, too, so I could feel fine about taking it easy for a little bit now.

✻   ✻   ✻

Morning, the next day.

Come winter, it was so painful to get out of bed. I had worked pretty hard yesterday, and I could feel the desire to just lie around building up within me. But still, time waited for no one, so I forced myself to throw the blanket off and stand up.

"Good morning."

For once, Rit had risen before me. She'd been tending to the herbs in the garden, despite the chill. Her fingers were pale, so I wrapped them in my own. Her hands felt like ice.

"So warm."

Rit sat next to me with a smile.

She was also working hard. She didn't have alchemy, preparation, or any other production skills. Still, her spirit magic helped to encourage plant growth, and it kept pests away.

As a princess, Rit had been trained in etiquette, but she had also frequently slipped out of the palace and interacted with common people. This experience had made her into someone capable of dealing with customers in whatever way worked best for them.

What's more, as a first-class adventurer, she knew as much about medicines as the average apothecary, if not more. From the perspective of someone who used the remedies, she could explain the less well-known aspects like side effects or what happens when people with blessings that have various resistances take certain curatives.

Since the advice was coming from Rit the hero, even adventurers who lived on the northern side of town had started going out of their way to patronize our store.

That Rit had trained the promising new rookie, Al, had also contributed to her outstanding reputation. When Al had registered with the Adventurers Guild, one of the shadier adventurers who had often taken jobs from Bighawk had gotten into it with him. However, Al had used his small stature to his advantage, lured the man into a narrow alley, and beaten the ruffian down with his dulled training shotel.

While there was a marked difference in blessing quality between Weapon master and Warrior, defeating someone with a higher level than him had gotten Al lots of attention. This, in turn, had spun rumors about just how great his swordsmanship master—Rit—was.

Several adventurers and guards would look for a time when there weren't any other customers and buy something while asking Rit for a bit of advice. The paintings that Rit had brought over were well received, too. One day, an aristocrat from downtown had come by looking to purchase several of them at quite the price. I'd refused, of course. Yet that visit wound up attracting a few more wealthy customers who bought medicines from time to time.

The reviews for the new anesthetic had been positive so far. After the whole incident with the Devil's Blessing, people were paying more attention to things like addictiveness. This created an increase in my sales.

The demand for heaters was steadily growing, too. While there was a limit on the number of orders I'd take each day, it was getting to the point that I had to leave tending the shop front entirely to Rit in the morning.

The sales were a far cry from back when I had first opened the shop. If things kept up, the herbs I had gathered in the mountains only a short while ago would be exhausted.

Rit had pointed out yesterday that it might be better to just make a deal with a farmer somewhere and set up a full-on herbal garden.

It took a fair amount of knowledge to cultivate medicinal plants, but the mountain provided a steady supply for me in the meantime. However, if you measured based on output per land area, herb crop still paled in comparison to what you could do with vegetables that had been selectively bred for agriculture over hundreds of years. That meant adding a percentage to whoever agreed to do the growing.

"But even with that, it would probably be cheaper than buying from the Adventurers Guild."

Ever since I had stopped bringing them medicinal herbs, the Adventurers Guild was always low on supplies. Because of that, the price of medicinal plants was going up. Though, apparently, the price they were paying the adventurers to gather them was still the same. If they handled things with a little more cleverness, I thought they'd turn a better profit. Yet the Zoltan Adventurers Guild didn't seem possessed of much interest in those sorts of things.

"Welcome!" I could hear Rit's voice from the front of the shop.

I smiled a little and then focused on the preparation work I had at hand and left the counter to her.

*   *   *

We had pizza for lunch today.

With Rit watching the shop, I started in on the cooking a little bit early. I flattened the dough I had prepared this morning and spread a fair amount of tomato sauce around it.

"I had been wanting to try making a seafood pizza."

Zoltan was located at the mouth of a river, so it had good access to all sorts of seafood.

First, I laid some sliced cheese on top of the layer of sauce. Then I spread some de-shelled clams, sausage, and tomato slices across the cheese. Lastly, I added a little more cheese to top it all off.

While I was baking it in the oven, I grated some of the potatoes we had gotten from the farmers to make a thick potato soup. The base was a broth made from ground meat and vegetables that I had made many times before.

I salted the leftover sausages for a little flavor and then fried them in a pan. They swelled up nice and round as they cooked through. When I took a bite to test the taste, there was a nice little pop to it. For the finishing touch, I whipped together a salad with tomato and lettuce. All I was doing was chopping them up a bit, so it wasn't incredibly complex.

Opening the oven, I took the pizza out, and the smell of cheese and clams filled the kitchen. The cheese was nicely melted, and the top had browned.

I sprinkled a little bit of chopped parsley over it and put a bit of red pepper on a small plate on the side for spice.

Rit came in right as I was putting the finishing touches on the meal.

"That looks delicious! I'll take it to the living room."

"Sure, thanks."

Rit deftly lined the plates of food on the table. It was just second nature by now.

""Let's dig in,"" we said together.

Rit grabbed a slice of the pizza and munched into it. Seeing her smile as she held her hand to her cheeks like that, I gave myself a little pat on the back today.

✳   ✳   ✳

We'd finished lunch and were enjoying some herbal tea.

"Oh yeah," Rit began. "Apparently, there was a breakout at the prison this morning."

"A breakout?"

"Yeah, one of the guards who came in to buy some medicine mentioned it to me."

"Huh, that's surprising. Did they already catch the escapees?"

"Apparently, it was a pretty serious thing. The guard said that whoever it was had destroyed a jail wall using some kind of special explosive that hardly made a noise."

"What?" I asked in disbelief. That certainly sounded like a pretty big deal. "Hmmm. Was it some people connected with Bighawk, maybe? It seemed like the Thieves Guild was glad to have him off their hands, but maybe the faction behind him there was bigger than it seemed. A large-scale jailbreak is probably going to mean things will be a bit more on edge around town for a while."

"The thing is, it apparently didn't turn out like that," Rit corrected.

"What do you mean?"

"It was the inner wall of the prison that was destroyed, and the intruders timed it to happen during breakfast. Lots of convicts tried to escape, but the outer wall was still intact, so none of them got out."

"That's pretty mysterious."

"Supposedly, there were prisoners who tried to climb the outer wall or take some of the guards hostage, but they got everything under control in the end. There was only one escapee."

Ah, a feint. That one person must have been the target from the start.

"It doesn't really make sense, though. Was there truly anyone that important being held there?"

"It was that guy you cut. He was in the infirmary there. You know, the alchemist who kidnapped Al?"

"Oh, him, huh…"

Rit was referring to the little man who had used adhesive bombs.

Despite how he'd seemed, he possessed a high-level Alchemist blessing and had, albeit indirectly, put Rit in a tough spot with his sacrificial bomb. Letting him remain free could be dangerous.

Then again, he'd been injured for a while before being taken to the prison infirmary for treatment. Cure would have closed his wounds, but he still won't be able to move much for a while.

"Hopefully they catch him soon."

"Yeah."

With that, we ended our break. Rit returned to the storefront, and I got up to head back to the workshop. The two rooms were in the same building, only a few meters apart, but Rit gave me a hug and a gentle kiss on the cheek, reluctant to be even that far from me.

*   *   *

During that same morning, Ruti and Tisse were walking through the north district.

Their breath was white in the cool morning air.

Tisse was rubbing her cold fingers together, wishing she had bought one of the Loggervian heaters that had recently gone on sale in Zoltan.

"Since it's a prison, they undoubtedly have some kind of anti-magic defense in place. I'm sure an invisibility cloak won't be much use."

Countermeasures for illusions like invisibility magic and the like would have been the first thing anyone would've implemented. An answer for every kind of magic was extraordinarily difficult. Still, by targeting specific lines of magic, it was possible to deal with the common threats while keeping within the local budget.

"We'll stick with what we planned to start," Ruti whispered.

Recently, Tisse's view of the Hero had changed. It was true that she had some blind spots when it came to common sense, but she was by no means thoughtless or incapable of planning. Indeed, she had managed a meticulous preparatory investigation that even an assassin like Tisse had to acknowledge as thorough.

Ruti had researched the prisoners' and guards' daily schedules the other day and gathered the data necessary to determine what timing would be best for her and Tisse's infiltration.

After discussions, the pair had settled on the plan that seemed most likely to succeed without significant collateral damage, though it would draw attention.

Unlike the stone wall that surrounded Zoltan, the outer brick barricade enclosing the prison was quite tall, and sharp spikes were lining its top. Clearing it would be difficult without having a blessing like Roof Crawler or Wyvern Rider that had access to the skill Essence of Jumping. Unbothered, Ruti drew her hole-filled goblin blade.

"Martial Art: Boulder Splitter."

When Ruti brought her blade down, the wall was cleaved apart as easily as if it had been made of wet paper. The two of them quickly and quietly slipped through the square hole that had been gouged into the barricade. Once they were through, they pushed the block back into place in the wall. Because the cut from the Martial Art had been so sharp, there were no fragments missing, and the wall fit back together perfectly. The traces of the slashes were invisible, barring a careful inspection. And it had all happened in under a second.

Up in the guard tower, there was a bored guardsman on duty to keep watch, but by the time he looked over in Ruti and Tisse's direction, the two of them had already snuck into the shadows.

✳   ✳   ✳

The bell for breakfast was ringing in the prison.

A guard was leading the prisoners standing around the tables in prayer before the meal.

There was a thump. The guard furrowed his brow but did not say anything.

"Kh, damn bug."

It was the sound of a bald-headed prisoner stomping on a big beetle crawling across the floor.

When he moved his leg, the insect's insides were stuck to his bare foot. The convict with burns on his face standing next to the bald-headed one grimaced at the sight of it and spat. A middle-aged bureaucrat imprisoned for corruption was standing across from them, looked fed up with their uncleanliness and lack of civility as he audibly scoffed.

"You got summin' a say?! Huh?!"

The bald convict who crushed the bug stared the middle-aged man down, but the former bureaucrat met the glare with one of his own.

The bureaucrat, despite his countenance, had a Grappler blessing. He'd engaged in illicit activity because his profession had not been well suited for his blessing. He had vented all the pent-up frustration from the urges he could not deal with in his job by going goblin hunting on days off, so he had a reasonably high level. He was confident that he could hold his own in an unarmed fight, even against an outlaw.

Meanwhile, the bald prisoner's blessing was Bar Brawler. He was a recidivist, having been incarcerated for starting fights on several different occasions. The most recent time, his trial had been finished in only a minute, and he was sentenced before even having a chance to speak. He acknowledged that this was just the sort of person he was, though, and he made his living day to day by either backing up someone looking to start a fight or shaking people down for money. It was not a way of life to be bragging to other people, but that was part of why he could not let it slide when he felt that someone was looking down on his strength.

The burned man standing next to the bald one had been a day laborer with the Warrior blessing. He had stabbed someone in a pointless scuffle, and unfortunately, the guy had ended up dying from it. The burned man had already been in prison for a year. The reason he had ended up in jail had nothing to do with his blessing. Whenever he saw the prisoners' foolishness, he just regretted everything.

The three of them had entirely different values and blessings.

The bald man finally leaped over the table as the middle-aged convict raised his hands and got into a stance.

Right as that happened, there was a loud bang. The three of them looked in the direction of the sound, jaws hanging open. One of them shouted, but when questioned later, none could be certain who that was.

At that exact moment, the three convicts with such differing circumstances all had the same thought.

"Outside!"

There was a big hole in the wall of the cafeteria. By the time the guard had come to his senses, the prisoners were all scrambling for the aperture. Everyone there thought they had heard an explosion, but that had been a misconception.

It was Ruti's fist that had destroyed the barricade. Humanity's strongest fist slamming into the wall had created a thundering noise that had resembled an explosion.

By the time the convicts had started running toward the hole, Ruti was already gone.

❋   ❋   ❋

The intruder casually sauntered down the hall of the prison's infirmary ward, unnoticed by anyone.

This infiltrator was strolling around the infirmary without drawing a second glance from anyone, memorizing the rooms' layout and their inhabitants—and all without using any magic. After examining every chamber in the structure, the intruder climbed up to a window with iron bars across it, and they slipped through the gap between the rods.

"Welcome back, Mister Crawly Wawly."

Tisse smiled when she saw her buddy return.

Mister Crawly Wawly waved a leg in response and then hopped onto Tisse's arm. Using her Spider Understanding skill, Tisse communed with the arachnid. Because spiders did not understand letters or words, the information came to Tisse as more vague images. However, Tisse had done much practicing on her own to be able to interpret those visions.

"Yes, I see. Thank you, Mister Crawly Wawly."

Mister Crawly Wawly raised his front legs as if to say "No problem!"

Because of everything going on with the attempted escape, all the guards had been summoned to deal with the prison riot that had formed. Only one person had been left behind at the entrance of the infirmary. And that one person had been knocked unconscious by a precise strike by Tisse.

"Skill: Decoy."

When Tisse activated her skill, a person appeared in front of her that looked exactly the same as the guard she had just rendered senseless.

Decoy was a skill that allowed her to make a copy of either herself or someone she touched. The duplicate couldn't move very far or speak, but it could carry out simple orders like "Walk back and forth along this path" or "Nod if anyone says anything to you."

The copy was like a balloon with nothing inside. It was actually a summoning skill, rather than an illusory one. This kept it from being exposed by anti-illusion abilities.

Tisse knew from experience that despite the copy's limited repertoire, it was quite capable of buying a significant amount of time.

The rest would be a race against time. It was another thirty minutes after the guards had put down the unrest before they noticed that Bighawk's coconspirator—an alchemist named Godwin—was missing.

✳   ✳   ✳

Ruti removed the gag in the man's mouth.

"Wh-who the hell are you?"

Having been dragged to a dark warehouse in the harbor district, Godwin was trembling in fear. Every time he moved, he clutched his shoulder wound in pain. He was no longer bound in any way, but he could tell that the two people there with him were far more powerful than he was. There was nothing to be gained by trying to resist.

Faced with that question, Ruti paused to think for a bit. "I want you to make Devil's Blessing." Eventually, she decided to just come out and say it.

"Devil's Blessing…"

Now understanding the reason for his kidnapping, Godwin's breath calmed somewhat.

I see, so they wanna sell Devil's Blessing? I didn't think there was any way I would escape a death sentence, but it looks like there's still some hope left.

Devil's Blessing was a medicine that rejected the faith and teachings of the holy church, so Godwin had been sure that he would end up on the executioner's block since he'd been the one who'd created the drug.

He'd been left with little hope of escape, and he had secretly been intentionally keeping his wounds fresh while in bed in the infirmary to stave off the date of his demise for as long as he could.

But I need a demon's heart to make Devil's Blessing. I can't do that without Mr. Bighawk. If they figure that out, I'll be useless to them. I need to buy some time to get them to take me someplace far away from here for safety.

Godwin's mind was racing desperately, searching for a way out of this with his head still connected to his neck.

Maybe I'll say that I can't get the supplies I need in Zoltan anymore? Some backwater place far away, without wanted posters. Or perhaps a city with a criminal network to take me in? Yeah, Mzali would work. They hire escaped slaves to work in the mines there. I could get a job making medicine for the people working in the mines and have a decent enough new life.

All that was left was how to explain things. Godwin was feigning doubt about how to respond to his kidnapper's request when…

"Here."

Ruti passed a paper to Godwin that immediately blew all thoughts of treachery from his mind.

"Th-this is the recipe for preparing Devil's Blessing?!" the alchemist shrieked.

How had these two young women come by it? And if they knew how to prepare it, why had they gone out of their way to spring Godwin from prison?

Intermediate Alchemy and Special Ingredient Handling were all that was needed to make Devil's Blessing. It required a certain level, but it was not so high that there was no one other than Godwin who could do it.

The reason Ruti had wanted him was that she did not have the knowledge of alchemy that a specialist like Godwin possessed. The Hero wanted someone she knew was capable of making the drug. Godwin, however, in his panicked state, could only see Ruti as some fearsome, incomprehensible, all-knowing being.

"Wh-why…?" The question was meant to inquire how Ruti had the recipe and why he'd been busted out of jail. However, Ruti misunderstood what Godwin was getting at.

"So I can use it."

For some reason, Godwin could not stop himself from shuddering as Ruti looked down at him with her cold eyes and announced her intent.

"O-okay! I'll do whatever you want! So please stop looking at me like that!" he pleaded desperately. A man who had lived his life in the dregs of society was cowering like a child.

*   *   *

"*Too many people know about Devil's Blessing in Zoltan,*" the imagined Gideon said, and Ruti nodded her head in agreement.

Since that Gideon only existed in Ruti's mind, a nod was enough to be understood.

"*And even without that, people will be on their guard around here with the uproar caused by breaking this Godwin guy out. You have what you need from Zoltan, so you should move to another location as soon as you can.*"

"*But first, we have to heal his wounds at least.*"

The injuries Godwin had suffered from the adventurer who had cut him down still hadn't recovered, and because of his efforts to push his execution date further into the future, the wound would cause problems if Ruti and Tisse tried to travel with him.

"*Can I just use Healing Hands to take care of it?*" Ruti inquired silently to the visage of her big brother.

Gideon shook his head at her question.

"*No, it would be best to hide the fact that you are the Hero from him, if at all possible. Healing Hands is a skill that only you can use. I doubt he's well versed in the Hero's skills, but if it can be resolved without blowing your cover, that would be best.*"

"*Yeah, you're right, Big Brother.*"

"—Hero."

Tisse's words broke in, causing Gideon to disappear. Ruti turned her attention to the world outside her mind.

The morning sun was shining through the window, and she could hear gulls squawking.

"Good morning."

"Good morn— …Right, you don't sleep."

"Correct."

"So then, what shall we do today?"

"Go buy some painkillers and cure potions."

Tisse paused in thought for a fraction of a second before quickly realizing Ruti meant that they were for Godwin.

Currently, Godwin was bound with rope and had been stowed in a large box inside the warehouse. If he ran away, he would just be executed by the Zoltan authorities. Regardless, his spirit seemed entirely crushed by Ruti's imposing pressure, so he was behaving himself.

"Understood. Do you have an apothecary in mind?" Tisse inquired.

"I heard there is an apothecary for sailors here in the harbor district."

"The one here doesn't seem to have a good reputation. Apparently, they sell low-quality medicine because their clientele is all seafarers who aren't around very long, so a bad reputation does not matter. They've been warned by the Merchants Guild several times to address their problematic business practices, but…," Tisse trailed off, the implication in her silence apparent.

"I see. Do you know of one?"

"Ah… Well, there is another apothecary in the central part of the town… Or maybe…" Tisse hit her hands together as if remembering something. "Heaters."

"?"

Tisse frantically tried to explain as Ruti tilted her head slightly.

"Yes, the word is that there's a druggist in this town who is capable of making Loggervian heaters. The store's reputation is good, and I've heard their medicine works quite well."

"Loggervian heaters."

The battle in Loggervia. The image of Ruti's big brother injured from the fighting, the warmth of his body as she held him close, the strong squeeze as he hugged her back... The Hero blessing, weakened by Devil's Blessing, was unable to hold back the pleasant emotions welling up in Ruti's heart.

"Let's try there," Ruti decided with a nod.

The working-class district and harbor area neighbored each other.

Ruti and Tisse left their inn near the docks, walked a little while through a wooded path, and arrived at a modest but well-built wooden shop. The sign over the door said RED & RIT'S APOTHECARY.

"This is the place."

A bell rang as Tisse opened the door. Because it was a druggist's in the working-class part of town, she had pictured a shabby interior, but the inside was far tidier than expected. Shelves lined the walls, displaying different medicines. There were also little cases of herbs placed around the interior to keep any miasma away, and they spread a faint, refreshing aroma.

There were several lovely paintings on the shop walls, and in the middle of the room was a sculpture of a winged angel with loving eyes. Tisse did not know much about the arts, but she felt like the gentle colors of the paintings, and the angel statue, instilled a sense of peace.

Cure potions and various other magic mixtures were only available by asking the person at the counter. The product list on display next to the statue was unexpectedly comprehensive. It seemed the rumors about this apothecary being reputable were true.

There was a single man behind the counter. He was arranging the remedies on one shelf while chatting with a half-elf man.

"That's—?!" Tisse gasped. It was the incredibly skilled adventurer she had met at the *oden* stand.

She was just about to warn Ruti when...

"Big Brother!!!"

"Ruti?!"

What Tisse saw in the moments that followed was a scene that shattered every preconceived notion she had ever held about the Hero.

There were tears in Ruti's eyes, but she had a sparkling smile as she spread her arms and hugged the man tight. The man was shocked but still caught Ruti as she came flying in.

"I missed you! I was so lonely!"

The tense aura Tisse always felt around the Hero was gone. As Ruti smiled and cried in the man's arms, she was just a girl.

Chapter 3

- - - - - - - -

The Hero Wept

My little sister was in my arms. The sibling I thought I might never see again—and certainly not before the demon lord was defeated.

"Big Brother!!!"

Ruti's arms wrapped around my back and squeezed me tight. She was smiling as tears ran down her cheeks.

Both Gonz, who was standing next to me, and the *chikuwa* girl from the other evening who had come in with Ruti, were slack-jawed in shock. I was going to have to explain this all somehow, but…first things first.

I gave Ruti the biggest hug I could. I mean, I was glad to see my little sister again, too—from the very bottom of my heart.

Ruti seemed to have finally calmed down after a little bit, so I gently pushed against her shoulders, and she released me without fighting it. Her expression had gone back to normal, too.

She was still grinning, but it was one of those expressions of hers that probably looked like a blank face to people who didn't know her well.

"Big Brother…you were completely wrong."

"…? Say what?"

"I didn't feel anything special about Ares at all."

Did she mean that time when Ares put his arm around her when I left?

"Really? I could have sworn—"

"You were wrong." Ruti cut me off with an uncommonly forceful tone compared to how she usually spoke with me. It was her way of rejecting what I'd been about to say without giving me any room to argue, so I just let it go.

"I understand. I guess I just misunderstood."

"Right." Ruti looked sad as she corrected me.

I see. So she and Ares weren't really like that... On the one hand, that made me a little happy, but on the other, it was depressing to realize that Ruti had been left with no one to count on after I'd left.

...I should probably explain things to Gonz and the chikuwa *girl, but how do I even begin to provide an excuse for all this?*

"'Big Brother'? So does that mean she's your little sister, Red?"

"'Big Brother'? Would you perchance be Mr. Gideon?"

"Gideon?"

"Red?"

Gonz and the *chikuwa* girl were both looking confused.

Argh, how do I deal with this?

✳   ✳   ✳

Rit was out getting food for dinner. I was going to have to outline a few things to Ruti before she got back. At the same time, Gonz needed to be set straight as well.

He wasn't tight-lipped by any stretch, but he could at least tell the difference between things that shouldn't be shared and things that could be.

"Hmmmm."

I flipped the sign on the shop to CLOSED. There was no way I could handle customers in this sort of situation.

"Ummm, you first, Gonz," I decided.

"So what's the deal?"

"This girl is my little sister. But please don't tell folks about her yet. I'll explain everything later, so if you could just keep this to yourself and head back now, I'd appreciate it."

"No problem. I dunno what all you have going on, but it's clear enough to see that it's not like the two of you hate each other or anything," Gonz said, being accepting with a big smile. "It's a special thing, havin' a little sister."

Like I had Ruti, Gonz had Nao. The two of them got along really well, and he even treated her husband, Mido, like family, too, to say nothing of how much he doted on Tanta.

Gonz stood up and patted my shoulder.

"Also, Little Miss. Red…or maybe his real name is Gideon? I don't know the story for any of that, but he's a great guy and real dependable. In this part of town, everyone counts on him. He hasn't done anything bad, so don't you worry about stuff like that."

"Okay," Ruti replied with a nod. However, it looked to me like her expression was ever so slightly troubled.

✳   ✳   ✳

The only ones left in the living room were me, Ruti, and the *chikuwa* girl—Tisse, her name was. She had an Assassin blessing, and she'd joined the Hero's party to replace me on Ares's recommendation.

I thought my duties and those of someone with an Assassin blessing were pretty different, though…

"Where to even begin…," I wondered aloud.

"Big Brother."

"What is it?"

"Are you living together with someone?" Ruti inquired as she glanced around the room.

Ugh. She'd caught on before I'd even had a chance to say anything.

There wasn't anything in the room that would give Rit away.

However, the vase of flowers and the style of some of the housewares betrayed that there was someone who shared this place with me. It's a little nerve-racking to have to tell my little sister as much, though.

"Yes, I'm living with someone."

"...I see."

"She'll probably be back before long. You remember when we were in Loggervia? Rizlet, the princess who used shotels and traveled together with us for a little while?"

"Yes, Rit."

Ruti seemed a little sad as she nodded.

I guess I truly had been misunderstanding things when I thought she had gotten closer to Ares.

Around the time when she set off on her journey—and really ever since she was little—she only had eyes for me.

"Anyway, I guess you'd deserve to know how I ended up here. I imagine you heard from Ares that I had withdrawn from the party to scout out the enemy."

"After that, Yarandrala started accusing Ares of killing you, so he explained that you had run away."

Dammit, Ares. Couldn't keep your word, huh? Not that I had any right to complain since I had abandoned my team.

I filled Ruti in on everything: Ares telling me to leave because I was holding the party back, the despair, drifting out to Zoltan, opening an apothecary...and how I started living with Rit.

"I intend to stay here together with Rit like this. And I expect we'll get married eventually."

I got a little tense when that word crossed my lips.

Rit was a princess, and while I was a knight, I was a commoner by birth, so all I had to my name was a low-level, nonhereditary peerage. It wasn't really an appropriate relationship in terms of status, but Rit and I were both resolved to relinquish our titles if we needed to.

"I see."

Ruti could tell from my expression that I was serious. She just nodded quietly without comment.

"I'm sorry for just disappearing like that."

"...Ares is the one at fault. But..." Ruti looked me straight in the eyes. "I'll silence Ares. So it's okay, right?"

"..."

"Rit can come, too. Let's travel together again, Big Brother." Rit sounded like she was pleading with me. My heart was aching.

I had thought that Ruti had found someone else to rely on besides me. Ares, Danan, Theodora, and Yarandrala had their foibles, but they were all comrades who had mastered the paths they had taken, and they were all stronger than I was. Ares's magic, Danan's fists, Theodora's spear and miracles, and Yarandrala's ability to control plants outdid anything I was capable of. Even without me, I thought for sure they'd have found their own ways to support Ruti...

"The party doesn't work together without you, Big Brother. I can kick Ares out if you want. But we need you."

Ruti explained how poorly things had been going for her team recently. Ares had tried to do the jobs I had been doing by himself and failed. Danan had gone off to search for me, and Yarandrala had left the party after thinking that I had been killed. Tisse had joined to take my place, but that was three losses with only one addition.

"..."

I had thought that Ruti had been making good progress on her quest when I'd heard she and her party had defeated Gandor of the Wind. But nothing about the Hero's journey was going smoothly. Just like Rit had feared, there had been significant problems after my disappearance. And if Ruti was saying that she wanted me to come back, that meant there was still a place for me in her group. If I wanted, I could go back to those days of adventuring again.

But... But even so... I...

"I'm sorry, Ruti. I've already found a reason for me to stay here."

It wasn't just Rit. This store, this slow life, they had become my reason for living. Answering the modest requests of the residents of Zoltan...the way they could get so happy from a heater to fight the winter cold...it made me happy.

Zoltan was already my home.

"I see," Ruti responded quietly.

It was almost like she had half expected my reply.

"In that case, I'll live here, too." My beloved little sister stated her determination to stop adventuring just like I had.

It was a selfish thing to say. It meant turning her back on the battle that would determine the fate of the world, but could anyone really rebuke her?

What was there to say? What could I tell her?

I was consumed in a bitter vortex of thoughts. Yet that didn't trouble me in the slightest. The more important thing was that the girl before me was suffering such unbearable sadness.

It was soon after that when Rit came with a bag of groceries.

"I'm back! Are you there, Red? Why did you close the shop?"

I frantically dashed out of the living room and into the storefront.

"I'm here. A…guest has stopped by. They're in the living room."

"A guest?"

The floorboards creaked behind me. Someone was watching from the door behind me. Not that I had looked back to see, though…

The bag of groceries Rit was holding dropped to the floor with a thud. She gasped and seemed to be at a loss for words.

"Um, yeah, my little sister is here."

Even without looking, it was easy enough to tell who was at the door to the living room from the expression on Rit's face.

"It's been a while," Ruti said quietly.

*　　　　　　*　　　　　　*

There was a clink as I set the cups of coffee I had prepared on the table. The room was so quiet that the sound was almost deafening.

Not good.

Rit and Ruti were both focused pointedly on the drinks in front of them, making no effort to look across the table. Tisse's gaze was fixed on a little spider resting on the back of her hand. The arachnid was glancing all around as it made a gesture that almost seemed like it was trying to comfort Tisse.

"Um, Ruti, where are you staying?" I asked, if only to break the unease.

"An inn in the harbor district."

"The harbor? Wouldn't the taverns in the north or downtown be a bit nicer?"

"It's fine."

"I see... So what are you going to do? Do you want to stay here tonight?"

There was a spark of excitement in Ruti's eyes at that, but she immediately looked down again.

"No. There's still something we need to take care of in the harbor district...but the day that's done, I would like to be together with you."

"Got it."

Something to take care of...?

"I hadn't gotten a chance to ask yet, but why are you in Zoltan?" I inquired.

"One reason was to look for you."

"For me?"

"Because you're necessary to defeat the demon lord."

The way Ruti had looked when she first saw me, and then when she'd said she was going to live here...and now admitting she had traveled to Zoltan in search of me... None of it really added up.

"And the other reason was to seek out someone else."

"Who?" I pressed.

"A knowledgeable person who was hiding away in Zoltan. He has some information that is necessary to defeat the demon lord. But I already found him, so that part's been taken care of."

"I see."

"Um!" Rit finally spoke up. "...What are you going to do, Red?"

Oh yeah, Rit wasn't here for that part.

"I'm going to stay here and keep running this store with you, Rit."

"Really? …But…" Rit glanced over at a despondent Ruti.

"You don't have to worry… I'm going to live in this town, too," Ruti stated matter-of-factly.

"H-huh?!"

"We're going to head back for today."

"'Head back'…?"

Ruti stood up. *Weird.* I had felt like something was really off since earlier, and that niggling sensation refused to go away. Whatever was going on with Ruti didn't seem entirely bad, but I couldn't trust that it was wholly good, either.

"Big Brother."

"Feel free to come by whenever. I'll be here."

"I was just about to ask that." Ruti smiled bashfully as she lowered her head slightly. I gently patted her head.

"Mm…"

"I still haven't gotten to talk with you enough. We both have so much to discuss…all the things that happened after I left."

"Yes, but this is enough for today…" Ruti met my gaze. She looked satisfied.

"It's fine. I have lots of time to spare now."

From her spot next to me, Rit was stunned at the sight of Ruti's visible smile.

*   *   *

As quickly as she had appeared, Ruti left, taking Tisse with her.

Rit and I sat at the table, deep in thought.

"Hey, Red. Is this all okay?"

"What?"

"Um… Maybe it's a bit weird for me to be saying this, but…Ruti really needs you."

"Yeah."

"In that case, I can't help thinking…maybe it would be better to just go with her." Rit looked pained.

"For the sake of the world, huh…"

If I was being honest with myself, I couldn't deny that my heart was wavering. A part of me was unsure, especially after I'd seen how sad Ruti had looked.

"We should talk again. Ruti and I—and you and Tisse as well. All four of us."

"Yeah."

This wasn't a problem that could be quickly resolved. We were going to need some time. There would probably be plenty of people who would criticize the Hero for abandoning her quest. However, if anyone was guilty in all of this, it was me. Ruti had not done anything wrong.

Even if she had been forced to bear the fate of the world on her shoulders, Ruti was still just a seventeen-year-old girl.

✳   ✳   ✳

Having left the shop, Ruti walked away quickly and then groaned as she pressed her hand against her chest.

"M-Ms. Ruhr?!"

Tisse frantically dashed over to her.

Ruti took a vial of Devil's Blessing out of her pocket and drank it one gulp.

"I shouldn't have said I would stay here," Ruti whispered as a cold sweat formed on her brow.

An intense urge from her blessing was pummeling the poor girl. Devil's Blessing was supposed to lessen such impulses, but the world's most powerful blessing would not let the Hero toss away her mission without a fight. It resisted with an overpowering desire for justice, and a pain like Ruti's heart was caught in a vice.

"I have to weaken it further."

"Ms. Ruhr…"

Tisse was uneasy. She could tell that something was off about Ruti. She had not journeyed together with the Hero for very long, but she could tell that the other young woman was acting abnormally.

"Kyaaaaaah!" someone cried out.

Tisse immediately readied herself, but Ruti had dashed off even faster than the assassin.

On the outskirts of the working-class neighborhood, there was a road running along the irrigation channel that functioned as the line between it and the harbor district. There, a high elf woman had been pulled to the ground by her hair.

"Who the hell let a goddamn long-ear sell stuff here?!"

An *oden* cart had been toppled nearby.

The various things that Oparara had been working so hard to cook were mercilessly strewn all around, and the two men—their cheeks flushed from alcohol—were grinning as they stomped on the food.

"Stop it!"

"This here's a human town, ya hear? Freaks like you showing their face in public'll give us a bad name."

Human supremacists like them could be found just about any-where. They were generally denounced by most humans, too, but even still, there were enough of them to form their own little communities in most places.

A twisted sort of pleasure warped the roughnecks' faces after seeing Oparara's face swollen from the beating…

However…

"Huh?"

It only lasted for the blink of an eye. The next instant, a girl was standing before them with her fist cocked back for a punch. The man it was aimed at didn't even have time to curl up and protect himself.

"Grgh?!"

The air was forcibly knocked from his lungs, and he was hit with an agony like his insides had been trampled flat.

Ruti had punched him while being careful to hold back just enough so as not to kill the ruffian. Still, that restraint was not out of any sense of mercy. She had carefully modulated her strength to barely keep him from passing out while still ensuring he would feel the worst possible pain.

That one blow had struck the man with injuries that he would carry for the rest of his life. The drunk man crouched over, holding his stomach and groaning as tears and drool covered his face.

"Wh-wh-what was that?!"

The other roughneck panicked and tried to run away, but Tisse had already cut him off.

"O-outta my way!"

He thrust his arm out to knock her aside, but Tisse just caught it and used it to send him flying through the air.

"Ugh!"

Slamming him to the ground, Tisse pinned him using his elbow and gently jabbed a finger into his side.

"Ugh— Uggggggggggggghhaaaaaaaaah!"

He wailed pathetically as he received a firsthand lesson in the ways an assassin destroyed a humanoid body. It was an attack designed to cause significant pain without leaving any visible traces.

"The *chikuwa*... What a waste."

Seeing the food on the ground that the human supremacists had been stepping on, Tisse added a bit more force behind her finger.

∗   ∗   ∗

By the time a pair of guards arrived on the scene after all the ruckus, the two thugs had already been dealt with. Tisse and Ruti handed the shamefully sobbing men over to the authorities.

"They'll never make that mistake again," Ruti stated.

Tisse nodded in agreement.

"Thank you both for your help."

From the looks of it, the Zoltani guards were also pissed off by the men's random act of violence, so they didn't comment on Ruti and Tisse's *aggressive* response. Instead, they chose to leave the young women with a word of gratitude.

"Phew."

Tisse felt a small sense of satisfaction. It was rare for an assassin like her to be able to help people like that. While uncommon, it was not at all an unpleasant feeling.

Meanwhile, Ruti's reaction was almost the exact opposite. Her shoulders slumped a bit.

"Th-thank you! You saved me there!" Oparara walked over, a wet towel pressed against her cheek where she had been struck.

Seeing her face like that, Ruti placed her right hand on the high elf's cheek.

"Ms. Ruhr!"

Realizing with a start what she was about to do, Tisse tried to stop her, but Ruti did not listen and activated her Healing Hands.

"Eh?!"

Oparara was shocked. In an instant, her pain was gone. Her swollen face had shrunk back to normal.

"I still can't avert my eyes from people in need."

"Ms. Ruhr…"

"Sorry, even though it was so important to avoid using my skills…"

"N-no, it's fine… I'm sure what you did was right."

Right, that is what it was to be the Hero.

Tisse could accept it. She even felt a little bit of pride at the fact that she was standing on the side of righteousness.

Ruti was staring at her right hand, the one she had just used to save the weak and lay the strong blow. The impulses that had been torturing her minutes earlier had vanished after rescuing the high elf. And as time passed, the Devil's Blessing would start taking effect.

The reason she had run when she heard the shout was because she had thought that she would be able to ease the urges of her blessing.

In a soft voice that no one else could hear, Ruti asked her blessing:

"Is this really right?"

*   *   *

My name is Tisse Garland. I'm one of the Hero's comrades, and I have an Assassin blessing.

It is currently evening. I just came back from giving the alchemist Godwin, who we have confined in a warehouse, dinner.

The plan had initially been for us to escape Zoltan during the night, but the Hero found her brother, whom she had been searching for in this town, so the plan changed.

It seems like she is considering staying in Zoltan. However, it is also still necessary to have Godwin make the medicine.

Godwin is too well-known in this town...

We would need to provide an alchemy workshop near enough that the Hero could reach it from Zoltan while also keeping Godwin confined so he doesn't run away.

Difficult. That was the simplest way to put it.

If we had just a few more people, I could imagine a few separate ways we could accomplish that goal, but we only had the two of us. It was my first time in Zoltan, so there weren't any people I could trust here. There wasn't even a branch of the Assassins Guild. If push came to shove, I would guess that her brother Gideon was trustworthy, but...

"This is really quite the conundrum."

"Yes," Ruti said, nodding in response.

"Might it not be better to go to a different town until we've acquired more of the medicine? We could return to Zoltan after that."

"I know that."

"Eeep?!" I recoiled instinctively at the sullen aura emanating from the Hero. She was just sitting in a chair in thought, but it had such a powerful impact.

It had seemed for a short while like the force of her presence had softened a bit after meeting Gideon, but that was clearly not the case.

"There's a place I would like to check out tomorrow. In the meantime, we have about a week, so it doesn't have to be the top priority, but I would like to find a hideout."

"I—I imagine we could make something work for that long, but…a place you wanted to check out?"

"Apparently, there are ancient elf ruins on the mountain near where we left the airship. If the facilities are still intact, it would likely be sufficient for our hideout."

When had the Hero gotten ahold of that information?

"Supposedly, wood elves also used to live near that peak, and I've heard that useful plants grow all around there."

Odd. I had never heard of wood elves having lived in the vicinity of ancient elf ruins. But that was probably just due to a lack of known examples.

Wood elves held the belief that nature operated on a cyclical structure. Their structures were one with the natural world, so after they disappeared, the shaped trees continued to grow until all traces of the wood elves had disappeared. At least, that was what my teacher at the Assassins Guild had taught us.

There might have been other wood elf settlements built near ancient elf ruins that had just become unrecognizable with the passage of time.

"If the ancient elf ruins are still intact, that would probably be sufficient for a hideout… But why…?"

Why was the Hero going so far out of her way in order to remain here in Zoltan? Seeing her serious expression, I couldn't bring myself to finish my question.

Scary…

A tiny leg tapped my shoulder. Mister Crawly Wawly was tilting his head.

What is it? Mister Crawly Wawly was trying to say something.

Don't think so much about it? No, maybe don't overthink it? And also, really look?

It was rare for Mister Crawly Wawly to push me so insistently in order to communicate. He started restlessly moving his two front legs, trying to communicate.

I was a little bit nervous. Mister Crawly Wawly was trying his best to get something across to me, but I couldn't comprehend him at all.

"What is it?" I asked him to try to understand better, but he just kept transmitting the same vague image. I couldn't understand. It had been a long time since I'd had this sort of problem.

My efforts with Mister Crawly Wawly commanded all my attention, distracting me from the Hero.

"Tisse."

"Hn?"

Without me realizing it, Ruti had walked right up to me. Surprisingly, her gaze was not directed at me as I froze in shock. She was looking at my shoulder. She was staring blankly at Mister Crawly Wawly.

The Hero stretched her hand out toward my shoulder. My thoughts froze. Fear and panic tore through me. I must have done something to anger her.

Not Mister Crawly Wawly!!!

Before I was aware what I was doing, I had leaped backward and drawn my sword.

My teeth were chattering. It felt like a fire was burning inside my head from the terror of drawing my weapon against an opponent I couldn't hope to defeat.

The Hero stopped moving with her hand outstretched, still expressionless. Her gaze was fixed on me.

It was probably just a short moment, but to me, it felt like an eternity.

"…You have it wrong," the Hero explained as she looked at me. "I know that creature is your pet. I wasn't going to hurt it."

What was she talking about? My breathing was ragged, and though I tried to listen to Ruti, I couldn't comprehend what she was saying.

"I've seen that spider moving its legs around a lot next to you. I've even spotted it giving you insects that it caught…"

The Hero continued to say things like that while I stood there, still trembling and with steel in hand. A small shadow leaped into my view.

"Mister Crawly Wawly?!"

My pet spider leaped to the ground and raised both of his front legs, doing his best to make his small body to look bigger as he stood in front of me.

"Wh-what are you…? Huh? 'Really look'?"

What am I supposed to be looking at…?

Mister Crawly Wawly was desperately flailing his small body, telling me over and over to peer harder.

And then…I finally saw it.

"This is a misunderstanding. I would never do something like that."

Who was standing in front of me? The Hero. The person who bore humanity's most powerful blessing, who shouldered the burden of saving the world, who lived for the sake of what was right, and who was feared by all her comrades. However, when I really examined her, all I saw was a puzzled girl who had upset her friend but had no idea how.

Our perceptions of the situation were off. I had drawn my sword in terror and gone into a stance ready to fight, but to Ruti, while she did not understand why, she could tell that she had upset me somehow.

The Hero was too strong, and she had become too far removed from the rest of us…murderous intent or hostility from an ordinary person did not register to her. It was almost like how a young child could be genuinely angry, and to adults, it just seemed charming.

And the reason I had finally managed to recognize that disconnect that had left her isolated all this time was because I had finally really looked at her.

Thinking back now, I understood. When we had been talking on the airship, the reason the Hero's expression had shifted from time to time while she was looking at me was that she had been noticing Mister Crawly Wawly and smiling, just like I did. That night, what she had been looking for outside was a small pet of her own like Mister Crawly Wawly. That was all.

Ruti seemed at a loss for what to say…

"I'm sorry I don't know what I did to upset you, but please forgive me. I didn't mean to, and I am very remorseful."

So she just apologized.

There was a clatter as I dropped my sword. Terrible guilt gripped me as I wondered why I hadn't noticed any of this sooner.

I squatted down, and Mister Crawly Wawly jumped onto the back of my hand. He conveyed an image to me.

Apologize? Yes. I should.

I walked over to the Hero—to Ruti. Her shoulders twitched ever so slightly.

I took a deep breath.

"No, I should apologize to you. I was the one who misunderstood. I'm truly sorry."

"I see... So you're not angry?"

"No, I'm not angry at all. Are you angry, Ms. Ruti?"

"I'm not."

"Good. But— Um...when you want to pet him, could you please just tell me first?"

"I understand."

I held out Mister Crawly Wawly to Ruti. She brought her left hand close.

Hop.

Mister Crawly Wawly leaped nimbly from my hand to Ruti's. And then he waved his right leg at her to say hello.

"...What is its name?"

"Mister Crawly Wawly."

"Crawly Wawly?"

"*Mister* Crawly Wawly. The *Mister* is part of his name, too."

Ruti looked puzzled for a moment and then looked at my pet spider.

"Nice to meet you, Mister Crawly Wawly. I'm Ruti."

She smiled gently as her eyes narrowed.

My name is Tisse Garland.

I have an Assassin blessing, and now I am the Hero's friend.

*   *   *

The ancient elves—the first race, said to have ruled over the lands at the dawn of the world, between the time of the gods and recorded history.

There was the first realm where fairies and spirits dwelled. The warmth of springtime enveloped that land all year-round, and the immortal, unaging fay danced and sang. It was a paradise of never-ending pleasure. Those that dwelled there never knew pain or conflict. As a result, every day was incomparably blessed and filled with joy, so they had no desire to change anything.

Because it was a paradise, the first realm was one of infinite stagnation. After observing that first world for eons, Almighty Demis began to feel displeased with that inactivity.

That was when Demis created the second realm—this realm.

On the first day, the cosmos was created.

On the second day, the heavens, the sun, the moon, and the stars were created.

On the third day, the insects, animals, and plants that would become sustenance were created.

On the fourth day, the monsters that filled the world were created.

On the fifth day, intelligent creatures like elves, dragons, and demons were created.

On the sixth day, the ancient elves were created in the image of a particular fairy from the first realm that was said to be the most talented. Their destiny was to rule over this realm. Humans were created in Demis's own image.

On the seventh day, with his work done, Demis rested, and during that night, the Asura were born.

On the eighth day, the Asura appeared to greet God, and God became angry, declaring, "I did not create beings such as you."

*   *   *

According to the holy church's book, that was how everything had been created. The dwarves and orcs who lived on the dark continent were subspecies of elves. The goblins who proliferated throughout the world were also the descendants of an elven race that had originated on the dark continent. High elf scholars argued that goblins and elves were entirely unrelated, but that remained a fringe theory.

The term *ancient elves* was a modern convention. In the oldest copies of the Church's books, the creatures created on the sixth day were referred to as merely elves, while the word used for the elves devised on the fifth day was actually *fay*.

There was significant debate among scholars about the relationship between modern fay and elves, but the current consensus was that elves were a breed of fay. They were a sort of higher kind, distinct from arch-fay and possessed with the ability to establish an advanced culture. That is merely the leading theory, though. In this world where theology and biology intertwined, it became difficult to determine what was correct.

To clarify the current understanding of elves:

- ✖ Ancient elves (extinct)
- ▼ Wild elves
- ✖ Fays that were equivalent to elves
- ▼ Wood elves (extinct)
- ▼ Half-elves
- ▼ High elves
- ▼ The original dark elves on the dark continent
- ▼ Dwarves, orcs, goblins

That marked the consensus of the elf studies field.

None doubted that the ancient elves possessed a more advanced civilization than is even seen in modern times. However, their exact nature is still shrouded in mystery.

Scholars comparing the elven coins that could raise the level of one's blessing temporarily to the secret medicine of the wild elves that temporarily lowered one's blessing level led to the belief that the ancient elves had analyzed and gained some more profound understanding of blessings.

Some among the clergy asserted that the ancient elves had incurred God's wrath for their arrogance and been destroyed.

The true reason for their ruination was unknown. However, both the first demon lord and the first Hero had been born in that era. The story of the latter's triumph over the former had been passed down for centuries.

In other words, the first Hero had not been a human, but an ancient elf.

In which case, just let a modern elf be the Hero, Ruti thought as she cut through the clockwork giant that stood before her. The slash elicited an unpleasant metal screech.

✳ ✳ ✳

Ruti and Tisse were venturing into the ancient elf ruins that resided in the depths of the mountain where Red went to gather medicinal herbs.

Thankfully, portions of the old structures were still intact.

The upper level had been disturbed by chimeras and adventurers from Zoltan looking for ancient elf treasures, but the contraption for moving to the lower level was untouched.

The device had powered down for a time because the mana crystal it ran on had lost its charge. The gem had been replenished by absorbing magic power from the surroundings over the intervening years. Thus, restarting the lift to the chambers below wasn't much of a hassle.

Having explored ancient elf ruins countless times before, Ruti controlled the magically powered lift with practiced ease as she and Tisse moved to the lower level of the abandoned structure.

This new floor was populated by the familiar clockwork monsters that infested all ancient elf sites. Ruti and Tisse were searching for the clockwork mother who controlled all of the lesser mechanical enemies.

"Phew." Tisse wiped the sweat off her brow. Unlike Ruti, who seemed unconcerned as she fought, Tisse had found herself in peril more than once during their battles, and she was looking tired.

It's not just the defensive clockwork knights. There would only be a single clockwork giant right before the clockwork mother in other ruins, but we've already encountered four of them. There were even a few clockwork destroyers, and they're supposed to be used in invasions, not guarding. I definitely saw some underwater clockwork leviathans, too... What the heck is going on with this place?

Tisse cursed it all in her mind. Despite the seemingly endless onslaught of mechanical opponents, she was able to continue deeper into the unusually menacing ruins because Ruti would take down anything that stood in her way.

Finally, the two girls arrived at the clockwork mother's room in the depths of the ruins. If they destroyed it, all the monsters it oversaw would stop functioning. Selling its scraps would net more than one hundred thousand payril, which was why taking on an ancient elf ruin was something of a get-rich-quick scheme.

I wonder if any adventurers would still be that excited after seeing this, though, Tisse thought after subconsciously recoiling back half a step at the sight before her.

The clockwork mother was a mass of gears that controlled all the other mechanical creatures in the ancient elf structure. And standing before it, as if to guard it, was a shining assemblage of metal—a clockwork dragon.

Unlike the other machine monsters that had screeched unpleasantly when they had moved, the dragon's body was elaborate—almost artful—in its construction. Its parts hardly made a sound as it moved. Within its body flowed burning tar, and the spark flickering in the recesses of its open maw evoked the image of a red tongue.

The creation was legendary, an ultimate weapon. Stories spoke of a device like this that the previous demon lord had restored. Supposedly, it was so powerful that it had killed some of the last Hero's comrades and forced that Hero to retreat in defeat once.

A cold sweat formed on Tisse's brow. Until now, she had never believed that clockwork dragons existed.

"Ms. Ruti!"

Tisse was going to suggest that they withdraw for the moment and get Gideon and Rit to help. It was too powerful for the two of them to face alone.

"It's fine."

However, Ruti appeared wholly unbothered. Her sword, the Holy Demon Slayer, hung at her side listlessly. Ruti did not even adopt a readied stance as she faced down the massive, artificial opponent created by the ancient elves.

＊   ＊   ＊

There was a mansion in downtown Zoltan.

It had once been the abode of a summoner, but they eventually joined up with the Mages Guild of another town and left Zoltan behind. The structure was one of the few buildings in Zoltan that had a basement equipped with magical defenses.

The manor gave off a creepy vibe, dissuading most from taking an interest in it. This left the place cheaper to rent than its neighboring homes. It was a perfect demonstration of how Zoltan was behind the times when it came to magic.

"It suits my needs just fine, though."

Bui, the dark-skinned young swordsman, set the report he had finished reading on the desk he was sitting at.

The documents contained information on the wood elf ruins that existed around Zoltan.

They had almost all disappeared as trees overran them, but Bui had hired investigators and the few available researchers in Zoltan to investigate what remained.

Bui had been tasked with finding a particular object that the wood elves had secreted away.

Unlike other wood elf sites, which had grown into their surrounding forests, this structure would have remained unchanged because it needed to stand watch over the precious item Bui was after. His investigation had involved eliminating potential places and narrowing down the object's location, and at last, he was finally nearing the end of his search.

"No wood elf structures remain around here."

Bui drummed his fingers on the desk with a sigh. His mission had become troublesome.

Protecting something meant keeping intruders out, and that meant a structure surrounded by walls. The damn wood elves must have sealed it away in something other than one of their buildings.

"Did they resort to their usual trick and hide it in a natural fortress? If so, then maybe at the bottom of the southern ocean or the Wall at the End of the World?"

While it was undeniable that either locale would be difficult for humans and demons alike to penetrate, there were aquatic creatures at the bottom of the ocean, and dragons, gugs, and other beings could survive the Wall at the End of the World.

Bui was searching for something that the wood elves would want to be certain no one would ever reach. Thus, it was unthinkable that they would keep it in a place where anything had a reasonable chance of getting through.

In which case, if it was a place in Zoltan that no one would be able to break into, then that left just one place.

"The ancient elf ruins."

The site was a collection of half-crumbled buildings protected by blessing-less geared warriors who continued to move even after thousands of years. Typically, the wood elves avoided the remnants of their now-extinct brethren. However, the fact that they had established a settlement on the same mountain as the ancient elves in Zoltan was practically a confirmation.

Bui stood up, checked again to be sure there was no one at the stairs to the first floor, locked the door to the basement, and then flipped a switch hiding in the nearby bookshelf.

A segment of the wall noiselessly slid away, revealing a set of stairs leading underground. Descending, Bui arrived in a small room with stone walls.

It was a hidden chamber with powerful magical defenses that had probably been the previous owner's secret laboratory. Bui opened the shelf at the back of the room that was locked by a magic key. Inside was a single large, sparkling gray gem.

Its unnatural glow inspired unease in those who beheld it, but Bui paid that no heed as he touched the stone and bathed in the ashen gleam.

The gem was a rare magic item called an *incubus heartstone*. By synchronizing a gray onyx with it and then burying that onyx in the ground, it would unleash a curse that robbed those nearby of their spiritual energy. It was an item that converted the stolen force it stored into magic power that could then be accessed by the one who owned the stone.

It was an item from the previous demon lord's treasure vaults and made the perfect tool for Asura demons. Without a blessing, magic was difficult for them to use efficiently on their own.

"Hmm? Is this all that it has stored up?"

The blanched light dimmed soon after Bui touched it, and it transformed into a dull, shabby stone. Bui concentrated, checking to see if the sudden dip in his spiritual energy harvest was somehow his fault, but that didn't appear to be the case.

"Did someone notice the curse already and implement countermeasures?" Bui groaned to himself. Even the fay should not have been able to block the hex. Still, whether he wanted to believe it or not, the magic power provided by the incubus's heartstone was far from enough for what he needed.

"This isn't nearly enough magical power to investigate the ancient elf ruins on my own."

He would need an accomplice.

Unfortunately, he was far removed from the demon lord's army's front lines. He wasn't able to call in support, and there were no adventurers in Zoltan who would be of any use.

"What should I do about this?"

Bui touched his finger to his temple as he slipped deep into thought.

He was entirely unaware that, at the exact same moment, Ruti and Tisse were already clearing the ruins.

*   *   *

Two weeks had passed since Ruti had arrived at my shop.

The following three days, Ruti had been away, but after that, she'd shown up regularly. She and Tisse registered as adventurers, and while they had not been incredibly proactive about it, they were taking quests to clear out goblins near the town from time to time.

The two girls were powerful. Clearing goblins was beneath them, to say the least. It seemed likely that the reason they took the quests was to stave off impulses from their blessings.

Exterminating goblins—humanoid creatures—who were attacking villages was the perfect way to deal with both the Hero blessing's urges to save people and the Assassin blessing's desire to kill people.

What's more, since all they were doing was fighting weak opponents, Ruti and Tisse were taking the quests without any concern for the number of enemies. Word had started to spread around town about reliable new adventurers as people saw them heading out to the goblins' hideouts like they were going for a lighthearted stroll and coming back after having destroyed it.

And...

"Welcome."

"Eep?!"

For some reason, the pair had come to help out at my shop today.

I had tried having Ruti stand at the counter, but maybe because of her inherent, powerful aura, customers reflexively screamed when she greeted them.

The reaction hurt Ruti, but it also taught me something new.

"Perhaps if you were able to smile a bit more, they wouldn't react like that?" Tisse proposed.

"Really?"

I had assumed that I was the only one able to notice that Ruti was sad over the patron's frightened reaction, but Tisse had recognized it, too. She'd even given my little sister some advice.

"Yep, if you can manage to smile just a little bigger, I'm sure it will be okay. Do you mind if I leave the counter to you for a little longer?" I asked.

"That's fine." Ruti clenched her fist slightly. She was determined to keep trying.

*   *   *

While Ruti and Tisse were tending the shop front, Rit was checking the count on the various medicines in storage and taking inventory.

We always kept an eye on our stock, but now was a good opportunity to be more meticulous since we had extra help. Rit and I had been talking recently about how it'd be a good idea to do a thorough check of what all we had.

"Doing okay in here?" I entered the storage room, carrying two cups of coffee.

With pen and paper in hand, Rit was doing her best to take count of the many medicines we had stockpiled.

"Argh! I give up! You made me lose track of where I was!" she shouted with perceptible despair.

"My bad, my bad. I'll help you out after this, so how about taking a little break."

"Yeah, I was getting a bit tired."

The two of us went to the living room and had a seat. We could hear Ruti speaking with customers out front.

"Do you want to go check on her?" Rit inquired.

"There's not much point in having her do it if I'm standing over her shoulder. That kind of thing will make her self-conscious."

"You know her well."

"She is my little sister, after all."

Rit and I both took a sip of coffee.

"Mmm, it's especially strong today. Plenty of sugar and milk, too. But it's still delicious."

I had put a little extra effort into the brew today. I used three fine metal filters and poured the hot water over coarsely ground coffee beans. Openings in the filters would get blocked by the beans, extracting the coffee more slowly. This left the drink very potent, so I'd added a fair amount of milk and sugar, too.

"There is herbal tea as a palate cleanser, too."

"Because this is a coffee to be enjoyed in the moment, rather than for the lingering aftertaste."

"Right."

"Thanks, it's delicious."

It was a way of making strong coffee to be enjoyed at a slow pace. The herbal tea beside it was for occasionally resetting the palate so you could appreciate that fresh first sip flavor again.

Rit and I relaxed, enjoying ourselves.

"That was great. Thanks."

"I'm glad you liked it."

Rit placed her cup down with a satisfied expression. The two of us looked at each other in silence for a few moments. But before long, Rit stood back up.

"All right, I think I'm going to go take over the counter for a bit," she declared.

"What for?" I asked.

"It's about time they got a break, too."

"In that case, I'll go."

"Nope," Rit refused with a grin. "I'm sure Ruti wants to be able to enjoy sipping her drink with you after all."

Rit left the room without giving me any chance to get a word in edgewise. I flicked one of the cups. It made a nice sound.

Even though she had kept the cost down, the dishes Rit had chosen were good quality ones.

"All right, I guess I should get some drinks ready for the two of them."
Putting the cups on a wooden tray, I headed into the kitchen.

✳   ✳   ✳

"Thank you both for your help."
There were three cookies and a trio of sweetened cups of cocoa set out on the table.
"Thank you."
"If I may."
Ruti's eyes sparkled as she took a sip from one of the mugs while Tisse decided to go for a cookie first.
"These are adventurer rations, right?" Tisse asked with a shocked expression. "It's...quite delicious."
"I mixed some nuts I gathered up on the mountain into it. They give it a flavor almost like cinnamon," I replied.
"Cinnamon...I've never had that before."
"Really? Then I'll make a cinnamon pie for tonight. Also, here, I soaked a bit of cloth in sugar water," I said.
"Huh?" Confused, Tisse cocked her head slightly to one side.
"I thought it might make a nice snack for that spider," I explained.
I nudged a plate with a bit of cloth on it over toward her. The arachnid hopped down from Tisse's shoulder. It raised its leg politely to greet me and then started to drink the sweetened liquid.
"So you noticed him. Thank you very much."
"That little guy? I mean, you seemed to be getting along so well with him."
"His name is Mister Crawly Wawly."
"Crawly Wawly?"
"The *Mister* is part of his name, too."
A tiny smile crossed Tisse's face at my reaction. Her outward expressions were relatively subtle, but behind that, she seemed to be a normal girl, just like Ruti.

"Big Brother."

"Hmm? What?"

"Is it okay to have lunch with you, too?"

I patted Ruti's head. I had just been talking about dinner with Tisse.

"Of course it is. That was the plan from the start."

"I see."

"And not just lunch. You're going to stop by for dinner, too, right?"

"Yes," Ruti responded with a smile. "The truth is: I love your cooking, Big Brother."

Ruti broke out in a natural grin. It was almost spellbinding. It was a lovely expression that immediately conveyed Ruti's feelings.

"Yep, I remember."

"Right!"

"Is there anything in particular you'd like to have?"

"...I want to drink honey milk."

"Got it."

My sister's request wasn't really what I'd been getting at—I'd been hoping to hear what she wanted for lunch. It didn't matter all that much, though. There was still an hour and a half left until lunchtime.

What goes well with honey milk?

At lunch, Rit, Tisse, Ruti, and I crowded around the table.

There were bacon sandwiches, potatoes gratin, and a salad made with the breast meat of a dragon chicken—a giant, bear-size bird—I had gotten some from the market's butcher, as well as onions, and topped it with a lemon-flavored dressing.

Naturally, we also had hot milk with honey, made the way Ruti had loved ever since she was a child.

"Thank you for the food."

Unsurprisingly, Ruti went for the honey milk first. With the first taste, her eyes gleamed, and then she immediately downed half of it in one gulp on the spot. The years had done nothing to change the way she drank it. I couldn't help but break into a smile from the nostalgia.

"Ah, this is dragon chicken, right? That's different," Rit commented as she partook of the salad.

It was just like Rit to notice something like that after a single bite. Dragon chicken meat had a slightly different flavor, but it was still basically just poultry. Judging by her grin, the flavor worked well for her, which was gratifying.

"Apparently, the farm missed it in their selection process, and one dragon chicken with a Beast blessing caused a mess and ran away. They got an adventurer to deal with it, but that left the butcher with a lot of poultry to offload, so it was on sale."

Unlike humans and elves, animals did not have many different kinds of blessings. They could be born with blessings like Warrior, Sorcerer, and Thief, but that was rare; only one in twenty. The remainder had Cattle or Beast blessings.

The former fostered a greater tendency toward cooperation and gentleness, while the latter tended to induce a dislike of flocking and more aggressive behavior.

Animals with the Cattle blessing were best suited for livestock, of course. The reason cows, pigs, horses, chickens, and goats were kept as farm animals was because they tended to have the Cattle blessing. It was rare for creatures like them to be born with the Beast blessing.

When it came to pets, it was possible to train an animal with the Beast blessing, but they weren't suitable as livestock for commerce.

It was standard for the owner of a farm to determine as quickly as possible which blessing an animal had and then have those with Beast blessings put down early. I had a few doubts about that method of handling things, but I didn't know enough about farm animals to really be butting into it.

The occasional broken fence wasn't the end of the world, but creatures with Beast blessings did occasionally injure other livestock or people. I guess addressing the matter in some form or another while they were still small was the only choice.

Hearing that the chicken meat had been from one with the Beast blessing, Ruti looked down at it with a severe expression for a moment before she began eating it.

I knew that Ruti wasn't much of a talker, but Tisse was a quiet one, too. She would say what was necessary to assert her thoughts, but that was all. After mentioning that she was enjoying the food, she ate in silence.

Judging from how her eyes were moving, she seemed to be paying close attention to what we were saying and how we reacted, but she was not the sort of person to contribute small talk to keep the conversation moving.

Tisse was more the sort who only spoke with a clear goal in mind. She'd use her words as tools to carefully and precisely convey her intentions.

Given that, the natural result was that Rit and I were doing almost all the conversing. We used the time to outline the sort of life we were living in Zoltan.

Compared to when I was a knight or part of the Hero's party, the day-to-day here was far more peaceful. Ruti seemed to be particularly interested as she listened to us.

"This is generally about how our day goes."

"From time to time, I have the shop to myself when Red goes out to gather herbs, though."

Rit was still calling me Red. We had spoken the night before about what to do about that—whether she should call me Red or Gideon when Ruti was around. We'd settled on keeping things as they were. While in Zoltan, we were just Red and Rit.

"Big Brother."

"What?"

"Is the place you get herbs that mountain to the northwest?"

"Yeah, it is."

"...In that case, I know the place. I'll get some for you."

"I'd certainly appreciate it, but are you sure?"

"Yes, it's fine."

"Got it. Then as long as it doesn't interfere with any of your own stuff, I'm happy to have the help."

Ruti nodded.

✳   ✳   ✳

I don't have dreams.

Winter had come to the forest, and the trees were barren in the cold. Gray clouds had blotted out the sky, and a cold, dry wind was blowing. My ears hurt, so I pressed my hands against them to warm up.

I was seven years old, and I was always by myself in the woods near the village.

It was only around a five-minute walk from home. If I listened closely, I could hear the sound of people going about their lives in the village.

I stayed in the woods, waiting for the sun to set—for the day to pass.

When there were lots of people around, there was no telling when someone would require help. The Hero couldn't refuse a person in need.

Hiding in my house was difficult, since my parents and I did not get along very well. My mother wove inside, and when I was around her while she was working, she would get into a terrible mood.

I didn't have any allies. Not anymore…

"*Ruti.*"

I spun around in surprise. That voice belonged to the person who I so longed to see, the one I was waiting for.

"*Big Brother.*"

I leaped into his arms as he spread them with a smile.

Usually, my mouth never moved, but my cheeks would just naturally relax when I was in his arms.

And seeing me grin, Big Brother would beam happily, too. Moments like that were blissful.

"*I was promoted to esquire, so I was given a week off to tell my family and take care of whatever preparations I needed.*"

My big brother had been scouted by the Bahamut Knights and had left for the capital. I had thought we wouldn't see each other for a long time, but he had risen from page to esquire in just half a year and had traveled all the way from the capital back to this far-off little village.

"I never had any free time because I was always busy attending to my superiors, but I'll be able to take some time off now. I'll come visit whenever I can."

"Really?"

"Really."

I welled up with joy and clung even tighter to him. He held me closer, too.

I would have liked to stay that way forever, but Big Brother gently released me after a bit.

"Shall we head back now? I haven't had a chance to say hi to anyone else yet."

"Okay."

I was a little disappointed. The two of us walked out of the forest, holding hands. His had gotten bigger and stronger since he'd left.

I didn't dream because I couldn't sleep anymore. At night, all I could do was walk through scenes from my past.

I could still clearly remember the warmth of Big Brother's hand holding mine back then.

I stretched my fingers out in the darkness of the night. Until just two weeks ago, I had thought that I would never feel his hand again. But now...

As I waited for the dawn, I smiled as I realized that I was looking forward to tomorrow.

The next day.

"Not that this is really the sort of place anyone would go for sightseeing."

"I see."

Ruti and I were walking around the working-class part of Zoltan.

The plan was to show her around. She still wasn't familiar with this section of town.

There were only a few clouds in the sky—great weather for walking.

As Ruti and I strolled along a path that had been worn into the ground by many before us, we spotted a bunch of kids waving branches and pretending to be adventurers as they ran around.

"Not so fast, goblin!"

"Grargh!"

The one pretending to be a monster was trying to sound menacing, I guess, but for some reason, he made a drake roar as he scampered about. The children seemed to be enjoying themselves. It was a familiar scene in this neighborhood.

One of the boys running around noticed me and turned around.

"Hey, Big Bro Red! Teach me how to fish sometime!"

"Sure thing. I'm a bit busy, but another day."

"Hurray! It's a promise!"

The boy raised his arms in joyful triumph. Then, as if realizing something, he made his best effort at a serious expression.

"Big Bro," the kid began.

"What?"

"You shouldn't cheat on Rit!"

"She's my little sister. She only just arrived in Zoltan." I grinned wryly as I tousled the child's hair.

"Cut it out!" He laughed as he shook his head.

"Heeey!"

"Ah, they're calling me. I'll see you later!"

With that, the boy ran back to his friends.

I was filled with warmth as I watched him go. It was a peaceful Zoltan morning scene.

When he was far enough away, Ruti tilted her head a bit.

"Are you certain it's all right to admit that I'm your little sister? Unlike that half-elf man from when we first met, that child will tell everyone he knows about me."

"I intend to keep your blessing and the fact that I'm the knight Gideon a secret. But you're my little sister. There's nothing bad about being proud of you. I don't see a need to conceal that."

"...I see..."

Upon hearing that, Ruti's eyes widened slightly. Then her cheeks relaxed a little bit, and she nodded slightly.

The two of us continued for a while until we came upon a familiar building.

"That's a sauna that we go to pretty regularly. It's run by an old man named Zeff. He's an interesting guy and a respectable artisan."

I was still delivering fragrance bags to him regularly. I'd worried that folks would get bored with it, but Zoltanis had truly taken a shine to a bath with herbal scents. It was just ten in the morning, but more people were going in than I would have thought.

"A sauna."

Ruti's gaze was fixed on Zeff's shop.

"Want to go take a look?"

It was a little bit out of the way, but there was no pressing reason I had to finish showing her everything today, either.

Nearly two years had passed since I'd left the Hero's party. Since we were making up for lost time, it wasn't such a bad idea to take a more scenic route.

At my suggestion, Ruti turned to look straight at me.

"I've never been in a sauna like this before," she admitted.

Back in our home village, there was a small lodge for smoking meat to keep it from spoiling. It also functioned as a community sauna. That was the best our little town had. There'd been no for-profit bathhouses or the like. And once Ruti had set out on the Hero's journey, there hadn't been any time for saunas in lands under attack by the demon lord's army. If we stayed somewhere after defeating the demons, it was usually the local lord's mansion or a palace. In such resplendent locales, we'd just used private baths there.

Thinking back on it, at least while she was with me, Ruti had never visited an establishment of this sort.

"So it's your first time, huh? Unlike the elegant spas they have in castles, this is a simple one that uses stones heated by a stove. It can get a little raucous with the other customers, but that's not such a bad thing, either."

"I'd like to try it."

"All right, then shall we?"

"Yes."

Ruti and I headed into Zeff's shop. Inside, there were several groups of customers who were enjoying a beer after their steam. It must've been nice to be able to drink in the morning.

"Welcome. Oh, Red, eh?"

Zeff's teeth flashed as he grinned and greeted us. The young man working part-time seemed busy delivering the drink orders and didn't have the opportunity to pay much attention to us.

"Looks like business is booming."

"All thanks to you. Don't think I've seen this young lady before," Zeff remarked as he motioned to Ruti with his hand.

"She's my little sister."

"Oh? You never mentioned having a little sister before."

Zeff gave Ruti a long, hard look.

Uh-oh, this might be bad.

"…gh." A cold sweat popped up on Zeff's wrinkled brow. His hand on the counter started trembling, making a noise as his fingers drummed nervously on the surface.

"Zeff, um…" I started frantically trying to think up an excuse.

However, Zeff just looked down, averting his gaze as he took a deep breath. "Phew, sorry 'bout that. I'm fine now."

"Ah, no, it's my bad. My sister is—"

"I've got no interest in prying into my customers' blessings or past. I'm sorry for bothering you, Missy."

Ruti looked a bit surprised as Zeff lowered his head. It might well have been the first time anyone had ever had that reaction to her. It was typical that people who saw the Hero found themselves incapable of ignoring her—whether they felt respect, fear, hatred, or whatever else. It was rare for someone to respond the way Zeff ultimately had, by pulling back a bit.

But that was the way things were in Zoltan. People here didn't pry into one another's lives.

"All right, two people, yeah?"

I placed two quarter payril on the counter, took the locker keys and towels, and then walked away.

"Okay, I guess I should explain things before we go in."

"Can I not just go in with you?"

"No, there are different rooms for men and women."

"I see."

Ruti looked dejected.

"But we can get drinks and some snacks after we finish in the sauna. It's not much, but let's have a little something together."

"Okay."

Then I outlined how to go into a public sauna. Ruti nodded along as she listened with her own sort of serious expression.

"That's the gist of it, at least. As for me, let's see, I was thinking of keeping it a bit short today and get out after twenty minutes, but what did you feel like?"

"I'll do that, too," Ruti replied.

"Got it. You should relax and not worry about time, though. I'll wait for you out here if you take a little longer."

"I'll be okay."

"Great!"

And with that, Ruti and I split up for a bit and went to our respective changing rooms.

*　　　　　*　　　　　*

Last time, Gonz and Storm had turned it into a competition, but saunas weren't the kind of place for an endurance test.

When I got out of the sauna, I dumped a jug of water over my head to wash off the sweat. The cool liquid felt great on my hot body. There were refrigeration units in a high-ranking noble's sauna to cool the water so you could enjoy the tranquil temperature of a lake in the middle of winter, but there was no way you would find a magical device like that in Zoltan.

But— Well, even without that, just plain water felt great when you were washing away the perspiration after a steam.

"That should be enough, I suppose?"

It was a little earlier than the twenty minutes I had said, but I changed back into my clothes and headed back into the hall.

A short while later, exactly twenty minutes from when we'd entered, Ruti came out.

"Over here."

Ruti trotted over and sat in the chair next to me.

"What do you want to drink?"

"Whatever you think is good."

"Hmm, all right… Then I guess let's get a mixed-fruit milk."

I placed the order with Zeff, and soon after, he brought two wooden cups of the stuff.

It was a tasty drink with a nice blend of sweet and citrus. Glancing over, I saw that Ruti was gulping hers down.

""Haah."" We finished and set our cups down at the same time.

"It's been so long since I could be together with you like this, Big Brother," Ruti said as her face relaxed. "We were always side by side when the journey first started. I was still weak, and you were always helping me. You taught me so many things."

"When we first set out, huh? Your blessing level was really low in those days."

"Traveling was fresh and interesting back then. And also, you were there."

"That brings back memories."

The demon lord's army had attacked our village, and Ruti and I had cleared the abandoned mine that the goblins were using as their base and then led all the villagers from nearby towns to take refuge there.

After that, we attacked the demon lord's army's camp, took care of a problem for a weapons merchant and got access to his weapon stores to gather gear, and then reclaimed our home with the help of the armed villagers.

The loss of such a small foothold was a paltry thing to the demon lord's army, operating on a continent-wide scale. Neither the forces of Avalon nor any powerful demons had bothered getting involved in such a small skirmish.

But even still, all the people who'd battled that day were serious. They were fighting to protect their homes and families, after all.

It was something much easier to picture than the fate of the world. You could say it was a bit less grand, but it was the adventure that had kicked off our quest.

It had been Ruti's first time outside the village, so everything she saw was new and different. I could still remember the first time she ever saw a unicorn. It was a tranquil scene as she brushed its white coat.

Unfortunately, even that was taken away from my sister as her blessing rose in level.

"Ah!" A young girl's voice suddenly brought me out of my thoughts.

A dwarf girl was looking at Ruti with wide eyes.

"It's the shaking girl!"

"Shaking girl?"

I was confused, but Ruti's shoulders twitched. The girl smiled like she was reuniting with her hero.

"That was so cool! The way you poured the water like *boom* right after getting out of the sauna, and then when you shook your body and the water went flying everywhere!"

In her excitement, the girl's voice grew loud. Other women who had been in the sauna with Ruti also commented on how impressive it had been, which caused a little bit of commotion.

Ohhh. Only one of the towels Ruti had was wet. I had just assumed she hadn't brought one into the sauna, but apparently, it was because she had shaken her body to dry off. It was a superhuman sort of feat.

Ruti looked down, seemingly uncomfortable. *Hmmm.*

"She's pretty amazing, isn't she? That's my little sister for you, though."

"She's your little sister?! So cool!"

The girl enthusiastically hopped up and down at that.

"Ohhh, you've got a sister, Red..."

The other people around us in the rest area seemed to relax a bit once they learned that the unknown entity was just the younger sibling of the guy who ran the apothecary.

"I've never seen anything like that before."

"She seems pretty strong. A pretty far cry from you, Red."

"She only recently arrived in Zoltan, so I was showing her around a bit."

"Ohhh, I see."

With that, their conversation shifted to the pet dogs they had, and Ruti and I slipped away after a brief introduction. Leaving Zeff's place, Ruti looked a little bit down.

"I'm sorry."

"What for?"

"I hadn't meant to make a scene."

I'm sure she had just been trying to dry herself as efficiently as possible. She still didn't seem to realize why it had drawn as much attention as it had, but she still felt guilty for drawing everyone's eye and causing problems for me when I was trying to hide my identity and just run an apothecary.

I gingerly brushed her blue hair.

"Ruti, you don't have to worry about anything here."

"But..."

"It's true that I'm keeping my past a secret, but none of them tried to probe any further about us, right?"

"Yeah."

"Even if you stand out a little bit, it won't cause a problem here in Zoltan. So don't worry about it. Just do as you please."

Ruti's red eyes stared straight at me. It felt like those ruby orbs were trembling slightly.

"You promise? It's really okay."

"Of course. I'm glad, even. I got to introduce everyone to my awesome little sister."

That was the truth. I had been considering going around town to everyone I knew and having them meet my sibling. The only holdup was that I still didn't have a clear grasp of what was going on with Ruti, so I wasn't sure how exactly I should introduce her.

"Am I really that great a little sister?" Ruti pondered in a soft voice.

It was very gentle, like she was just mumbling to herself, but there was no way I could have missed it.

"You're adorable, kind, and straightforward. I'm proud to be your brother," I declared firmly.

Ruti's cheeks flushed so subtly that anyone else would have missed it. She was embarrassed, and that was cute, too.

"All right, shall we continue the tour? How about we go check out the market next?"

"Okay."

Ruti held out her hand.

Whoa, that's nostalgic.

I took it, and the two of us walked through the neighborhood.

*   *   *

I could feel Big Brother's warmth as we held hands.

Today, it wasn't my blessing that was pulling me along, but Big Brother's arm. And that made me so unbelievably happy.

"Big Brother."

"Hmm? What is it?"

"Nothing."

He chuckled quietly at my silly response. That expression of his was more precious to me than any treasure I had ever held.

Ahhhhh, this is bliss...

If I could have just one wish granted, it would be to have this day last

forever. But it was God who forced the Hero blessing on me…so who should I be asking to grant my wish?

Unable to think of anyone, I kept the wish tucked away deep in my heart.

*   *   *

That night, Rit, Ruti, Tisse, and I had dinner together. Ruti's face was as flat as always, but she still managed to convey that she enjoyed the meal with every fiber of her being.

"Oh yeah, we have a bath here. Do you want to take a dip before going back to your inn?"

"A bath? Yes, please."

There was just no helping the fact that you almost never had a chance to take a proper bath while traveling. We would wash—cleanliness was important—but it was just a bucket of water and a towel most of the time.

There was a big old bell in our village that had been turned upside down that we used as a tub. Big might be something of an over-estimation, however, as it was only large enough for one child to fit in at a time. The adults in the village just washed themselves off with water and didn't get into the bath.

Our village widely believed that regular bathing made it harder for miasma to cling to you. Hence, the man who did the metal casting for the town acquired a discarded church bell and repaired it so that at least children, who were more susceptible to miasma, could take proper baths.

When we were young, Ruti and I had taken baths every three days or so.

"We used to wash together," Ruti commented nostalgically.

I guess she was thinking back to our childhood, too. For that bath, you would warm the water by stoking a fire directly underneath the bell. Unsurprisingly, the bottom of the bell would get incredibly hot, so wood boards were placed in the water. When you got in, you would sit on one of the planks, which would sink some, and you would have to be careful not to touch the bottom.

There was always an adult around, and for little children, their parents would help them, but because we both had gotten the hang of it at an early age, from around the time Ruti was two, I would get into the bath while holding her.

She would cling to me with her tiny hands. Our parents always complained that Ruti never cried, screamed, or laughed, but when we were in that warm water, her face would melt into a smile without fail.

It was so adorable to see how happy she was, so we had bathed together until we'd grown too large to fit in the bell. I'd like to believe Ruti had enjoyed that experience as much as I had.

"Can we get in together today?"

Phew, I guess it's safe to say she didn't hate it, then.

"Weeeell, at our age, we probably shouldn't be taking a bath with each other."

"I see." Ruti seemed to be genuinely disappointed.

Yeaaah… I mean, if we're siblings…? No, no, even then, we really shouldn't.

"In that case, I'd like to go with Rit."

"Huh?" Rit had been lounging comfortably in her chair, listening to us, but that caught her attention.

"Is that a problem?" Ruti pressed.

"…Hmm, no, that's fine. I had wanted a chance to chat a little bit with you anyway," Rit answered with a grin.

Ruti nodded with just the slightest smile.

I hadn't thought much of it, but Ruti and Rit really hadn't exchanged many words.

Way back when they had faced off in the colosseum that one time, Rit had wound up pretty bruised and battered. The experience might have left her feeling a little uncomfortable when it came to dealing with Ruti.

My sister was naturally a quiet sort of person, so if you didn't start the conversation yourself, she'd keep quiet.

This seemed like a good chance for the two of them to open up to each other.

"I see, then I'll go get the water warmed up," I said.

"Um?" Tisse called out. She was fidgeting her hands restlessly. "Would it be okay for me to join, too?"

It might be a bit tight for three people, but perhaps if I filled the smaller single-person tub attached to the main one?

"Sure, I'll get things ready, so just take it easy here for now."

As I got up, I caught Tisse closing her eyes like she was steeling herself for an encounter.

∗   ∗   ∗

On the seas. A first-class room in the high-speed clipper known as the *Sylphid*.

After being outed as a conspirator in the Devil's Blessing incident and losing to Red, Albert was lying weakly on a bed.

His head was throbbing in pain, and he felt an unpleasant sense of fatigue gripping his body. But even with all that, he was not dwelling on how terrible the situation was. Quite the opposite, he even felt a profound sense of satisfaction from the bottom of his heart.

The Sage, Ares, was beside the bed on which Albert was lying.

"Heh-heh-heh, I don't know what sort of mission you are pursuing, Ruti, but there's no way you can defeat the demon lord without me!"

Several days of using high-level magic had left Ares exhausted, but his bloodshot eyes still shone as he raised his arms and shouted his declaration.

Theodora was casting healing magic on Albert, who looked pale and sickly. Albert's eyes narrowed as he idly passed the time beneath the glow that was infusing him with life force energy.

There was no one in Zoltan capable of using healing magic of that level. Not Ria, the monk he had once formed a party with, nor even Bishop Shien who headed Zoltan's holy church could begin to compare.

But even with spells of this level, Albert was having his blood drained every day, which kept him from fully recovering.

After Tisse and Ruti had left in the airship, Ares, Theodora, and Albert, who had been dragged there in a stupor by the contract demon, had remained at camp for several days, just waiting idly.

When Albert found out that they were the Hero's party, he was excited. Long had he dreamed of joining up with such a glorious group. Even more than elation, though, he was ashamed and disappointed in himself for arriving not as a champion, but as a filthy criminal.

Things had since changed, however.

There was blood splattered around the floor at Ares's feet. It had been taken from Albert's arm. Distorted scars ran down his limb where it had been healed by magic only to be lacerated again, over and over.

As Ares concentrated, the blood seemed to squirm and form a figure of sorts that indicated a direction.

"There's no mistaking it! Ruti is somewhere in the direction of the Wall at the End of the World!" Ares's bellow resounded in the room.

Hearing the Hero's name, Albert's weakened heart started to pound in anticipation. However, while Ares and Albert grew more excited, Theodora's expression was distant.

"If she's on the other side of the Wall at the End of the World, then we've got a problem. Even if we go around it by sea, that would mean a voyage without any supplies. We're going to have to borrow a large carrack or a galleon warship. We aren't going to be able to keep up with an airship."

Ares seemed to have no intention of answering Theodora's concern. He just grinned as he stared at the crimson liquid on the floor.

"This blood still retains the power of the contract demon's accord! The one to go to the Hero's side! Our friend here has the ability to show us the way to Ruti! If I draw on this miracle, I can surely catch her!"

"Get a grip already," Theodora muttered as she beheld Ares's frenzied shouting with an icy gaze.

Ares swung around and glared at her with wide eyes. In those orbs was such a tremendous bloodlust that even Albert felt a chill run down his spine.

"What did you say?" snarled Ares.

"Milady left us behind of her own will. What meaning is there in chasing after her like this?"

"The power of Ares the Sage is necessary to defeat the demon lord! I'm merely doing my best for the sake of the world. Why are *you* here, though? If you really believe there is no meaning in pursuing Ruti, then shouldn't you just turn tail and run?"

"If left to your own devices, you would have already killed Albert here," Theodora spat back.

Ares's face warped as he lunged in and grabbed the woman by the cloak. "I can use healing magic, too! Mine is at least as powerful as yours, if not more so! Don't you dare forget: I've only entrusted this to you because you said you wished to do it!"

"You just don't understand, Ares," Theodora responded. Her tone of voice made it sound like she pitied him, which only served to vex Ares further.

"It's not enough to just have a skill that restores the wounded. If you can't empathize with an injured person and understand their pain on some level, then you can't actually perform the act of healing."

"Hah! What nonsense! Meaningless equivocation! Do you really think you can pull the wool over my eyes with such vague platitudes?!"

Judging that there was nothing she could say that would get through to Ares as he was now, Theodora merely shook her head limply and gently removed his hands.

"If it weren't for the fact that a life is at stake, this would be a good chance for you to learn from painful experience... Just leave Albert's healing and health management to me. I swear I'll keep him alive until you find Milady."

"Don't go thinking you can hold this over my head for a favor later. Not over something as trivial as this."

"I had no such intention. I'm merely doing what needs to be done, both as a cleric of no great importance and as someone who was once a comrade of the Hero who will save the world. We didn't fight all this way because of anyone's orders, to have someone owe us, or out of some desire for gratitude. We struggled because we wanted to save the world. At least that was why I fought."

Ares stared Theodora down with a tremendous glare, and then, as if to indicate he no longer wished to be in her presence, he stormed out of the room.

Theodora looked down at the blood on the floor and picked up a bucket of water to start cleaning. It had become a regular practice of hers recently.

"Shall I help you...?"

Theodora looked a bit surprised at Albert's offer.

"You don't have to worry about it. Just rest yourself."

"...Am I...? Have I been any help at all?"

Albert looked her in the eye. His gaze was weak, but his eyes were pure and bore no malice.

"I don't know. But thanks to you, we are getting closer to Milady. Whatever else might happen now, we will be able to determine the result for ourselves without relying on anyone else's decisions. And that is something we would not have been able to do with you, Albert. You have my gratitude for that."

"I see..."

A peaceful smile crossed his lips.

They would head toward the Wall at the End of the World next, taking the southern sea passage around it. That would put their vessel close to Zoltan.

Albert's missing right hand ached.

Seeing that, Theodora said, "Our next stop is the merchant city of Lark. We'll get you a prosthetic hand there. Lark does a lot of trade with the archipelago country. I'm sure they have prosthetics made by alchemists there. Even if you can't hold a sword, having a hand that can move again should ease the pain."

"But to slow your journey on account of me..."

"Don't worry about it. If it wasn't for you, we would never have discovered where Milady was. We can spare a little time," Theodora assured with a smile.

Albert glanced down at the stump that had once been a proper, full arm.

"He was mysterious, the man who severed my hand," Albert said, recalling the appearance of that D-rank adventurer with a bronze sword at his waist. He'd been strong. So much so that Albert couldn't even begin to guess at how badly he'd been outclassed.

"Why? Even with all that strength, why did he not become a hero?"

Albert wasn't expecting an answer. The quiet question was more directed at himself.

However, Theodora looked down at Albert with a hard expression. "People must try to live in a way befitting their Divine Blessing."

"That's what the holy church teaches," Albert added.

Almighty Demis bestowed Divine Blessings. Those who had been granted powerful gifts were expected to fulfill suitable roles. Theodora was a Crusader and a cleric of the sacred Last Wall fortress. Albert had expected her statement to end with some sort of remark about the church.

To his surprise, though, Theodora shook her head.

"However, Divine Blessings are not people."

"Huh?"

"People have free will. They have lives, dreams that they hope to achieve... Is someone with a blessing that could allow them to become a hero required to live their life as one? Are they not allowed to choose another path?"

"But that is what God wishes for them," countered Albert.

"Then why did God give people free will? If fulfilling the Divine Blessing's role is everything, what need would we have for choice?"

"That's... I don't know."

Albert was not a theologian, nor was he even a particularly fervent believer. He was not remotely equipped to debate a cleric like Theodora.

"My apologies. I'm actually looking for the answer to that question as well."

"Even you feel doubt?"

"I was left behind by Milady. I'm not nearly wise enough not to doubt myself after that," Theodora admitted with a bitter smile. "What was the name of the man who took your hand?"

"He called himself Red."

"Red, huh? I'd like to meet him," Theodora muttered quietly to herself as she took the bucket and brush for cleaning the blood on the floor and left the room.

Albert closed his eyes after watching her leave. Bereft of stamina, he quickly drifted off to sleep.

✳   ✳   ✳

There was a splash.

A single drop of water had fallen from the ceiling. Even though I was in a hot bath, for some reason, I felt a chill as I stared at the ripple it made.

My name is Tisse. I have an Assassin blessing, and I'm Ruti the Hero's friend.

Currently, I am soaking in a tub. To be frank with you, I love baths. I adore them so much that my fellow contract killers call me the bath reviewer.

During my journeys, I put together a guidebook that contained all the notes I had on public baths, hot springs, and sauna complexes in places I had visited over the years. It's considered a must-read by fellow Assassins Guild members preparing for excursions of their own. Murder was a rough line of work, and everyone wanted that one comfort that could bring them warmth.

A place where people generally stripped themselves bare and defenseless was the perfect spot for assassination, so my guide was also a proper resource for work. I'd written in notes about where to conceal weapons and the location of escape routes.

And from my perspective as someone who loved baths enough to write a book on them, this one…earned high marks.

Despite being for household use, there were two separate tubs, which was a big plus. The separate bath I was currently in was one in which you could really appreciate your personal space.

Society demanded that you communicate. That was no less true for assassins. In fact, precisely because killers had to infiltrate cities while always playing the role of a false identity, it was a job that often endured the stresses of social engagements.

No matter the time or place, you could never speak freely. You always had to control your communication, paying close attention to what exactly you might be saying and what sort of influence that might have on the job at hand. It was incredibly tiring.

I knew several assassins who had been working longer than me who were perfectly skilled as killers but had difficulty with the job's social aspect and could never make a name for themselves.

Because my master had drilled into me how to mask my emotions and thoughts properly, I could become whatever kind of person I needed. But it was not like I particularly enjoyed dwelling beneath a facade.

I'm trying to say that being able to soak myself in a private bath and enjoy a little space to myself as Tisse Garland made me incredibly happy.

That this bath used a pipe to warm the water was another point in its favor. If someone were outside stoking a fire, I wouldn't be able to help focusing on them. But with this tub, you could control the temperature by just getting a little bit out of the water and adjusting a valve.

"Four stars. It is just a little bit unfortunate that the bath is quite deep, so the water reaches my mouth while I'm sitting." Unfortunately, my comment was little more than a burbling sound that no one else could interpret.

I was short. Since I fought in a way that took advantage of precise strikes to critical points from behind rather than a method that relied on strength-based power, being small in stature was advantageous. Still, it also led to many inconveniences in my personal life.

Mister Crawly Wawly was currently dining on an insect that had been drawn to the humidity of the bath. Seeing him carefully holding it with his front legs as he ate it while looking so happy was endearing.

Haaah, I should stop trying to escape reality and face what's happening in front of me. I mean, it wasn't like there was an actual problem yet. It was just that both Ruti and Rit were in the same bath together.

Having watched her from up close recently…I could tell that Ruti loved her big brother Gideon. As in, she was deeply in love with him.

But Gideon and Rit both cared for each other. It was clear at a glance that they were head over heels for each other. And to Gideon, while Ruti was his beloved little sister, that was all there was to it. It was a different sort of affection from what he felt toward Rit.

"It's a nice bath, isn't it?"

"Yes."

There was no flow to Rit and Ruti's conversation at all as they sat across from each other. Ruti watched Rit without looking away, answering questions with few words, and not volunteering any discussion herself. Honestly, Rit was doing quite well to endure it.

Even if Ruti harbored no hatred for Rit, a person with ordinary nerves probably wouldn't be able to take sitting face-to-face with her. I had become the Hero's friend, and even I had a much easier time sitting next to her instead of directly staring her down. Honestly, I'm not sure Ruti felt zero anger toward Rit.

I had joined them in the bath like this to help ensure that nothing terrible happened in the worst case.

"Rit."

Finally, Ruti said something!

My heart was racing as I readied myself to leap out of the water at any moment if necessary.

Just in case!

"What is it?"

"Have you already taken a bath with my big brother?"

Going there already?! Urgh!

"Yes, I have."

And a merciless counter! Terrifying!

There did not seem to be any hint of turbulence brewing between them. Still, love was the sort of thing capable of pushing a person to murder. I knew that too well as an assassin, having seen all kinds of situations where someone felt driven to end another's life.

"I have, too. A long time ago, though."

"How was Red...Gideon back when he was young?"

"The same as he is now."

"So he hasn't grown at all?"

"No. Big Brother has always been cool." Ruti glanced down slightly. Looking closer, I could see her cheeks had turned a little red. "I used to be weak."

"Really? It's hard to imagine that with how you are now."

"It's true. My first fight was an orc hussar who attacked our village—no, that wasn't it. The first was when I went out into the mountains near our village to look for a child who had gotten lost."

"A lost child?"

"I was five years old, just a little kid myself. But I'm the Hero, and I couldn't ignore someone in trouble."

"Ah, the blessing's impulse...," Rit murmured with a serious expression.

The urges of a Divine Blessing were something that all who lived in this world encountered. The question of whether to live a life following one's Divine Blessing or to resist that and exist as you wished was one everyone struggled with. Most people chose the route their blessing pushed them toward. Resisting those intrusive impulses was a painful thing, and your blessing would grant you the skills necessary to live a life per the path it desired of you. Even so, there was no guarantee that was the sort of person you wanted to be.

While I was lost in that thought for a moment, Ruti began recounting her first adventure. She was far more talkative than I had ever seen her.

*   *   *

On the first day of spring, a girl who was not my friend ventured out to the mountains that were crawling with animals who had just woken from their hibernation and were wandering around in search of food. Somewhere along the way, she had gotten lost.

Big Brother had gone out to take care of something that day. I didn't have anyone else I could rely on. Father and Mother were not powerful enough to be going into the wilderness during that season.

I knew it was dangerous, but the Hero blessing pushed me, saying I had to go.

There was still a little bit of white snow left on the mountain. The river rushing so loudly was probably because of the snowmelt. I was only five years old. Even ordinary beasts were deadly opponents for me, let alone monsters.

All I had was one unreliable knife. I was shouting that lost girl's name as evening closed in, always moving to avoid anything that might be slinking after me. Noticing a presence, I turned around and saw a large wolf sizing me up. Perhaps it didn't desire to eat such small prey because it looked away from me disinterestedly and disappeared into the darkness.

However brave they were, a normal child would probably have screamed and run away at that. It was only natural. I didn't feel fear, though. I just acknowledged that the threat had passed and continued my dangerous adventure.

Shortly after dusk, I finally found the missing girl. Unable to navigate her way back, she had instead discovered a cave that seemed warm and was crying inside it. There were claw marks from a large beast on a nearby tree, and there was a powerful animal odor inside the cave.

If the girl had possessed Perception, then she would have noticed the enormous creature inside. The owlbear had already judged her to be its next meal.

Owlbears were at the top of the food chain in the mountains. Even the wolf from before would have fled from one. I imagine the only reason it hadn't killed her already was that it had just finished eating something else earlier.

The clever beast knew that human children died easily. The owlbear was letting her live so that it could consume her in the freshest state possible.

Although I had the Divine Blessing of the Hero, my level was still only one back then. I was just as much a kid as the lost girl. The enemy was an owlbear, something said to be unbeatable without at least a level of fifteen. The difference in strength between us was obvious. Still, I couldn't abandon her. I suppose you could call that a flaw with the Hero blessing. It didn't fear death and prioritized fulfilling the role of the Hero over survival. Not only that, it didn't even really register that such single-mindedness sacrificed something in return.

"Ruti!!!"

The girl noticed me and shouted my name as she ran over in tears, alerting the owlbear that another source of food had arrived.

"Guuooooooooh!!!!!" The great beast roared as it leaped out from the depths of the cave.

I held my knife in a backhand grip and readied myself. I knew my likelihood of winning was slim. If I failed, all that awaited me was death... I had just one chance. The owlbear charged and swung its claws down at me. It was too fast, so I couldn't dodge it. Because of that, I held my left hand to my chest and waited for that one moment.

The owlbear's claws ripped into my body.

"Healing Hands."

I should have been torn to pieces, but I was uninjured. Using all the power of Healing Hands, I had healed myself at the same moment its claws were gouging into my body.

I'm sure the owlbear never expected its prey to be uninjured. Using that moment where it was off guard, I slammed the knife into the owlbear's left eye as hard as I could. It roared in pain.

Too shallow...

Even though I had stabbed it with all my might, the knife had only pierced its eye. It was a deep wound; one could have been an eventual cause of death, but I had required an instant kill. My weapon needed to have reached the monster's brain.

There was a thud as I was sent flying through the air. The owlbear had flailed its arm and knocked me aside. Because it had not managed to hit me with its claws, I avoided dying then and there, but that was all.

My body rolled across the ground before finally coming to a stop. I desperately tried to raise my blade, but my arm was just hanging loosely… The bones were broken.

I had tried my best. There was nothing to be done.

And perhaps the blessing acknowledged that because it did not demand that I die on my feet. In its infinite mercy, in the end, it had allowed me to face death lying on my side.

Even if I didn't perish, all it would mean was that I would continue to suffer like this for people I wasn't even particularly close to. If I survived, I would continue to suffer for others, only to have them call me a creepy girl behind my back. My survival simply meant being used by those who secretly feared and hated me whenever it was convenient for them to ask for my assistance.

It was enough. I had lived for five years—not even that long counting from when I became aware of my surroundings. Back then, when I didn't have Immunity to Despair, that moment was more than enough to make me lose hope.

However…there was one person, just one, who did not demand my help. There was one who would always be there for me whenever I wanted help. One person who loved me just because I was his adorable little sister.

I could leave everything else behind without care: my parents, that village, even the world. But not being able to see Big Brother again…I couldn't take that.

And as that thought crossed my mind, the words slipped out of my mouth before I even knew what was happening.

"Save me, Big Brother!!!"

A blade slashed in like a bolt of lightning.

A sword cut into the left side of the owlbear's body, out of the blind spot from the eye I stabbed. The weapon slipped through the beast's thick armor of muscles and pierced its heart. The seven hundred kilogram monster perished with a single blow.

"Ruti! Are you all right?! You're so badly hurt!"

He did not pause to take pride in defeating an owlbear. He did not even glance at the tremendous feat he had accomplished. He just looked at my wounded body...and cried.

"I'm sorry for being late. I'm so sorry..."

"It's okay. You saved me, Big Brother."

I didn't mind the pain at all because the person in front of me would always be by my side whenever I was suffering. He would cry for me.

That made me happy.

When Ruti finished her story, she fixed her gaze on the ceiling.

Her flushed cheeks definitely weren't because of the hot bath.

"So it was like that for you, too."

Rit was looking at the ceiling as well. As if she was trying to remember something.

"When Shisandan killed my master and the royal guards and adventurers who had believed in and supported me, I was despondent. Even though I had gotten into such a bitter argument with you all about how we would protect our own country, at that moment, I couldn't help wondering if things wouldn't have been better if I had never been born. Since it was my fault that it had turned out like that."

"I see."

"And that was when Red saved me. He rushed in early before the rest of you arrived and faced off against Shisandan and fought for me. He pushed me to get revenge instead of stewing in regret for what had happened."

That must be something that happened during the fighting in the Duchy of Loggervia. Rit's eyes were closed as she recalled the scene.

"I'm sure you noticed it, too, Ruti, but there were countless times when we were in the bewitching woods when I was about to give up. It felt like we were wandering in circles, and even if we weren't, we spent a whole week in that forest... I couldn't help thinking that everyone in Loggervia might already be dead."

It was a dark story, but Rit's expression was bright and clear. The memory was painful, but it was also when Rit had met Gideon.

"Through it all, Red was there for me. He fought alongside me. He talked about trying to save Loggervia together. Deep in the bewitching woods, where the sun couldn't reach, I was okay because I had him. It was the first time I had ever felt like that."

Rit hugged her knees, hiding her mouth as she smiled.

Ahhh, I see. So that was the sort of person Gideon was.

It wasn't really a surprise that Ruti and Rit would both fall in love with him after those sorts of experiences.

Ruti cupped some bathwater in her hands and raised it. The water trickled out and back into the tub with a splash.

"Baths don't feel as good to me as they used to."

"Huh?"

"The reason that soaking in hot water feels good is that when you get into the tub, your body warms up, your blood starts circulating better, and tired muscles feel renewed." Ruti scooped up more water. The sound of the drips filled the room.

"I have immunities to all sorts of things now. Whatever extreme cold, or intense heat, my body temperature doesn't change. The warmth of a bath is no different. To me, it's nothing more than just a single piece of information that the environment around me is hot."

Drip.

"I don't get sick, and I don't feel tired. My body is always in optimal condition."

Drip.

"It's the same for food, too. I don't get hungry. I don't need water, either. I can taste flavors, but my body doesn't need nutrients."

Drip.

"The reason I think baths feel good is that I can remember the pleasant sensations of the past. I'm just re-creating the feelings from those memories."

Drip.

"The honey milk Big Brother made for me when I was little was the most delicious thing ever. It was sweet and gentle, and I felt like I could drink it forever. But the honey milk that I had today, even though it should have tasted better than it used to, didn't. But even so, I still have my memory of Big Brother's honey milk being wonderful."

Oh... So that was what had been aggravating the problem.

Ruti was humanity's strongest.

Ares and I, Danan and Theodora, and even Gideon—we were stronger than most other people. Yet even banded together, we wouldn't be able to defeat the Hero. Ruti would never again be able to experience the feeling of someone truly coming to her rescue.

Her feelings did not modulate as strongly as they used to because her blessing had taken the bulk of emotions that might harm her. Because of that, she could only experience love in the past.

...So does that mean Ruti can't ever love anyone other than Gideon?

Rit remained silent as well, shocked and unable to respond.

So this is the Hero's blessing? Humanity's hope, the Hero chosen by God, the world's most extraordinary power?

"When we were with you in Loggervia, I hated you, Rit."

"Yeah, I was definitely standoffish then. The whole 'Who would just stand by and let someone else save their home?' thing and all," Rit said, smiling wryly.

"I don't mean like that. I was jealous of you. Able to smile freely, to get angry, to cry...to love. I was jealous of you getting closer and closer to Big Brother...so jealous..."

There was a splash. Droplets of water were falling from Ruti's eyes into the bath.

"So truly envious…I hated you. And because of that, even though Big Brother and Ares said we should add you to the party, I didn't ask you."

"…Ruti…"

"Rit, Tisse…this is me." Ruti smiled so plainly that even Rit and I could tell.

"This is the Hero, Ruti… I just wanted to be you, Rit, not the Hero."

I had been wrong. I wasn't the right person for this. I had been worried about the incorrect thing. I hadn't understood what the real problem was. It needed to be Gideon here, not me.

He was the only one. Undoubtedly, he would have been able to save Ruti.

Ruti's forlorn smile was so tragic that it made me want to avert my eyes.

There was a tiny tap on my shoulder. Looking back, I saw Mister Crawly Wawly there.

"Huh? I'm wrong?"

He raised both his legs. If he had a voice, I'm sure he would have been shouting as loud as he could.

Don't give up hope! Just start now!

Mister Crawly Wawly was right.

A princess taken prisoner by the Hero blessing, unable to freely determine her path. Gideon was the hero who could save the princess. So then would that make me the mage to guide him?

Sensing a gaze, I saw that Rit was looking at me. The two of us exchanged glances. She nodded slightly, determination plain in her expression. Though it had only been for a short while, she had been one of Ruti's comrades, too.

We had two people and one spider to be the mages who guided the hero that Ruti needed. That would do for the cast of the story. The imprisoned princess had already suffered more than enough.

In that case, the next step was to lead Gideon to battle the evil dragon that had captured the princess and rescue her.

I didn't know what I could do to help Ruti, but Mister Crawly Wawly and I were her friends. Even if we couldn't see the goal in the distance, this was just the beginning!

The start of a story where we save the Hero, and everyone smiles in the end!

Interlude
- - - - - - - - -
A Story from an Alternate Universe

This is not a story of Red and Rit, nor is it a path that could ever have occurred. Even after millions of iterations, this route would never have happened so long as Ruti remained Ruti and Red remained Red. This is merely a story from an alternate universe that never existed.

It is a "what if" that presents what might have happened had the two of them remained faithful to their roles of the Hero and Guide for just a little bit longer.

*　　　　　　*　　　　　　*

Three years had passed since the demon lord Satan had commenced the invasion of Avalon.

In that short time, four countries had been destroyed, and most of the continent had fallen into the demon lord's hands.

People despaired, fearing that there was no longer anything left that humans could do to resist…but God had not abandoned humanity. There was a prophecy about the birth of a savior.

And then, a young girl appeared from a humble village and pushed the demon lord's advance forces back. Ruti Ragnason arrived in the capital bearing undeniable evidence of the Hero blessing. She destroyed he underground band of thieves that had the city in an uproar. Then she proceeded to the ancient elf ruins where the proof of the Hero was rumored to have been left behind by the previous Hero.

Ancient elf ruins. The dilapidated structures near the capital of Avalonia had an unknown spell sealing their entrance that repelled anyone who tried to enter.

Written in ancient elf script above the entry was the phrase *When he demon lord returns, the Hero shall arise again. We desire the Hero alone, and to the Hero alone shall we grant power.* When Ruti arrived, the gates that had barred the way for all others for hundreds of years opened.

✳   ✳   ✳

The giant machine, a clockwork knight over three meters tall, readied its ancient sword and shield and charged with a grinding screech.

"Watch out, everyone!" Ruti (the Hero, level sixteen) shouted as she readied her sword.

Ares (Sage, level fourteen); Kiffa, the prince of Avalonia (weapon master, level fourteen); Yarandrala, a high elf florist (Singer of the Trees, level twelve); and the frontier adventurer Gideon (Guide, level thirty-two) banded together and faced off against the clockwork knight.

"Martial art: Multi-Slash!" Ruti unleashed two quick strikes.

"Fireball!" Ares formed a sigil with his hands, summoning an explosion of flames.

"Martial art: Multi-Slash!" Kiffa loosed two cuts in rapid succession.

"Leaf-cutter!" Yarandrala formed a seal and attacked the enemy with a knife of foliage.

"Nrah!" Gideon slashed the opponent with a ceramic sword.

At the end of the fierce battle, the clockwork knight fell to its knees and stopped moving. Wounded from the struggle with the powerful opponent, the Hero's party healed themselves.

"The problem is even if you defeat these mechanical monsters, your blessing level doesn't go up any," Ares muttered.

"I guess that's because they aren't really alive," Kiffa responded as they looked at their defeated foe.

"But they will fill the coffers. The metal and other pieces that make up a clockwork monster can't be made anymore nowadays. My sword was created by shaving away at a clockwork armor plate," Gideon chimed in.

Walking up to the remnants of the mechanical guardian, Gideon pulled away the parts that looked like they could still be used and stashed them in his item box.

"That's the famed frontier adventurer for you," Ares praised as he watched Gideon efficiently sift through the remnants of the clockwork monster.

Gideon Ragnason. He was Ruti the Hero's older brother and an adventurer known as the best swordsman in the frontier. He had been with the party since the Hero had started her adventure. With his wealth of knowledge and experience, he was regarded as a cut above the rest, even by the other members of the party.

"The proof of the Hero should be through here, Ruti," Yarandrala said.

The group's goal was just ahead. Hearing that, Ruti's eyes gleamed.

"Yes! With this, the king will have to believe that I'm the Hero. With that, we'll gain the right to enter all the other countries and permission to call on the army for support. Then we can finally set out on the journey to defeat the demon lord!"

Ruti's voice was filled with excitement at the prospect of the quest finally beginning as she pushed deeper into the ruins with her comrades.

✳   ✳   ✳

With Ruti having managed to acquire the proof of the Hero safely, the kingdom of Avalonia officially accepted her as the Hero. To celebrate the return of this legendary savior, the king hosted an enormous banquet on the eve of the party's departure.

For a brief period, the band of mighty adventurers put thoughts of battle behind them and enjoyed the food and music.

"So this is where you two were."

As the banquet began to settle down, Ruti had realized that Ares and Kiffa were no longer in the banquet hall. She had gone looking for them only to find they were on the terrace of the castle.

"Sorry to have troubled you, Ruti. You didn't need to mind us. You should have just kept enjoying yourself at the banquet."

"What are you looking at?"

"The town," Ares replied as he gestured to the moonlit city. "There are so many people living out there. I think that is something incredibly precious, which is why I want to protect this place."

"Ares…yes, I feel the same. I can't stand by and let some demon lord or anyone else do as they please with our world!" Ruti responded.

Kiffa watched them, dazzled by the brilliance of their determination.

"I would have liked to have been able to go along with you. But I am soon to be married to Princess Serena, the daughter of the Duke of Dunwich. She is already here at the castle. She was even in the banquet hall tonight."

"Ah, that woman who seemed so friendly!"

"Yes. If she had been a disagreeable partner, I might have been able to consider ignoring my duty and leaving with you, but…she is a wonderful woman. I want to stay by her side and protect her."

"I think that's a magnificent thing, Prince. You should pay no heed to us. It was a short time, but our adventure together was fun."

"I enjoyed it, too! If my sword was of some use to you, then there is no higher honor." Kiffa smiled cheerfully, which caused Ruti and Ares to break into grins as well. Kiffa was the sort of man who could always find a reason to beam. Ares found himself a little bit disappointed, as he thought that Kiffa would unquestionably have brightened the mood if he had remained with the group.

"There you all are."

"Yarandrala."

The elf's silver hair swayed in the moonlight. She looked a little bit upset as she approached. "Argh, be a little more considerate, please. All of you just up and disappeared. Gideon was looking everywhere for you, Ruti."

"Sorry, sorry."

"You shouldn't make him worry so much."

Ares tilted his head at that. "You're always watching out for Gideon, aren't you, Yarandrala?"

"Wh-what'd you say?"

Ruti's eyes gleamed. "Ooooh, Yarandrala, are you maybe interested in Big Brother…?"

"N-no way! I'm just a little bit worried about him is all…"

"Oh reaaaally!" Ruti teased Yarandrala playfully.

Every once in a while, Ares would think that Ruti was reacting in a certain way, not because of her own feelings or goals, but because that was the response the person she was interacting with wanted to see. However, watching Ruti's eyes light up childishly when the topic of love came up, Ares was left chuckling wryly at himself for overthinking things.

"Um." Suddenly, a girl called to the four from behind.

Turning around, Ares saw a child, maybe ten years old, holding a bouquet.

"This is for the Hero."

"For me? Thank you!" Ruti smiled as she approached the girl.

"One of the maids here?" Ares idly used Appraisal. "No blessing? It can't be! Ruti! Get away from her!"

"?!"

At his warning, Ruti immediately leaped backward. The next moment, the girl's bundle of flowers exploded. It was a narrow escape. As the blast cleared, moonlight illuminated the girl's body, revealing torn clothes.

"A golem?!"

The child's body had been an artificial creation. The arms and legs moved with ball joints, and the cute smile remained as the mouth opened wide, revealing razor-sharp teeth.

"She evaded it…"

Three demons appeared from the shadows.

"Marionetteer demons! They've even infiltrated the palace?!"

Ruti and the others readied their weapons.

"I don't know whether you're the real Hero or a fake, but we can't ignore anyone who would dare call themselves that. This is where you die!"

The marionetteer demons attacked using their handmade golems.

* * *

"They were powerful enemies." Ares groaned as he pressed his hand against the wound where one of the golems had bitten into him.

"I'll heal you." Ruti activated her Healing Hands, and Ares's injuries quickly closed.

"There might be more. We need to warn the soldiers as soon as possible!" Kiffa had a grave expression. Yarandrala stood there deep in thought as she stared down at the demons' corpses.

"Why did they attack now? …It can't be!"

"Gaaaaaaaaaargh!" There was a tremendous scream and the sound of countless dishes shattering.

"The hall!"

The party dashed to the banquet hall. They could hear the sound of fighting from beyond the doors.

"Big Brother!"

Gideon was engaged in battle. Ruti reached out to open the entrance.

"Nrrrgh!"

"Gideon!!!"

The man's pained grunt was audible from beyond the closed doors. After that sound, there was silence. Yarandrala pushed Ruti aside and charged into the hall. Ruti and the rest quickly followed in behind her.

As they entered, there was a clatter as the stained glass window shattered. They saw a giant shadow disappear into the night sky.

"No! Gideon!" Yarandrala screamed as she clung to the man lying there.

The banquet hall was the portrait of a massacre. Many lay dead.

"Father!"

That included the king. Kiffa ran over to his bleeding parent.

The prince's voice trembled at the sight of his father's grisly state.

"No! He's already dead!"

"Ugh… Everyone…"

"Gideon! Thank God you're still alive!"

"S-sorry…I couldn't protect the king…"

"Don't talk! We'll heal you first…"

"No, there's no helping me anymore… Y-Yarandrala, call Prince Kiffa… I can barely whisper…"

Yarandrala gathered everyone over.

"P-Prince Kiffa, Princess S-Serena was here, too…"

"Wh-what?! Then…"

"She was taken by the demon… She still lives."

"Really?!"

"Wh-when I was fighting…the demon…dropped this." Gideon held out a shortsword.

"That's the crest of Desmond of the Earth!"

"The demon probably took the princess to Desmond… Gh…"

"I understand! You did well to tell us that much. It's enough. You don't have to push yourself anymore."

"Ruti…I'm sorry…"

"Big Brother…"

"I'm sorry I couldn't stay with you to the end…but you mustn't mourn me… You are the Hero who will save the world."

"But…I understand, so don't overexert yourself."

"Hah… Hah… And, Y-Yarandrala…"

"No, Gideon, please don't look at me like that…"

"I'm sorry…I couldn't keep my promise to see Kiramin with you…

Please, take this…" In Gideon's hand was a magic earring made from a tortoiseshell that had resistances to poison and sickness. He held it out to Yarandrala.

"I thought it would look good with your beautiful ears…"

"D-don't do this to me… I'm begging you… Don't give up."

"I pray…y-you find h-happiness… Gh…" With a final bloody cough, Gideon lost the strength in his arms. The earring dropped to the ground, bouncing gently.

"Noooooooooo!!!" Yarandrala hugged Gideon's lifeless body as she cried.

※   ※   ※

An hour later, Ruti and Ares were hurriedly preparing to set after the demon.

"We have to make haste."

"Yes, we must catch it before it can escape to Desmond of the Earth's castle."

Just as they finished packing, there was a knock on the door.

"May we come in?"

"Prince Kiffa? And Yarandrala?"

When Ruti opened the door, she and Ares saw Kiffa and Yarandrala standing just beyond it.

"Why are the two of you here? From the look of it, it's not just to see us off."

Kiffa tapped the short gladius at his waist. He had a round shield on his back. Yarandrala tightened her grip on the quarterstaff in her hand. They were both wearing travel clothes.

"It's my duty to rescue Princess Serena. Please allow me to accompany you."

"I'm closing my shop until I get revenge for Gideon. I'll never forgive the demon lord's army for stealing the man I loved away from me."

"Thank you both… It's reassuring to have your help!" said Ruti.

And so Weapon Master Kiffa and Yarandrala the Singer of the Trees both officially joined the party. Together with them, Ruti the Hero and Ares the Sage departed from the capital.

This was merely the prologue to the Hero's story.

Having lost her brother, Ruti endured her sadness and proceeded on her path without pause. The Hero, the embodiment of humanity's wishes, did not hesitate in the face of the tragedies that lay waiting for her, and she would surely never turn back until she defeated the demon lord Satan.

Oh yeah...

Seeing the teary determination in Yarandrala's eyes, Ares was suddenly struck by the realization that Ruti never cried, even though her brother had perished. If Ares had been a bit more sensitive to others' emotions, he would surely have noticed that Ruti's heart was empty.

Ares repressed the slight discomfort he felt and pushed onward. His duty was to save the world alongside Ruti, a hollow girl who felt happiness, sadness, and anger only when others expected her to and had no emotions of her own.

*   *   *

Back to reality.

*   *   *

"Sir Gideon! Please help!"

Prince Kiffa was guarding the king as he called out to me.

Facing down the flying demon that had flown into the hall, I drew my knight's sword.

"Things could get rough if it runs wild."

I started running as I tensed my arms. Ruti was following along beside me.

"Let's finish this in one shot. We'll attack at the same time."

"Got it."

Ruti slashed from the left, while I did the same from the right, cutting an X across the demon.

"Gaaaaaaaaaaah!!!"

The bloody cross-slice tore across the creature, and it collapsed to the ground.

"That demon was powerful. It might have been around level thirty-five."

If I hadn't trained up as a knight, it could have been pretty dangerous.

"Ooooh! That's the twin hopes of humanity for you! The Hero, Ruti, and Sir Gideon!"

The hall that had fallen silent at the demon's intrusion suddenly erupted into cheers.

"Are you okay?!" By the time Ares had opened the door and come dashing in, Ruti and I were being swarmed by the Avalonian nobility. The moment for questions like that had passed.

Ruti looked annoyed and started responding to the aristocrats with

half-hearted answers, so I forced a wry smile and desperately tried to cover for her.

It almost felt like Ares was scoffing in the distance, but I couldn't worry about him in addition to my sister.

Chapter 4

Heroes Gather in Zoltan

The next day, Tisse and Mister Crawly Wawly returned to the shop.

I had heard about what had happened in the bath from Rit.

"Thank you," I said as I bowed my head to Tisse and her pet spider, who were sitting across from me.

"There's no need for that. Ruti is a friend."

"That's the part I'm grateful for. Thank you for being her friend."

Ruti had never kept close acquaintances. The Hero blessing granted her a skill that gave everyone around her incredible courage. However, it also inspired awe that made those in Ruti's presence feel like she was some far-off being.

Even her comrades had kept a line that they did not cross with Ruti. I was the only one who had always stayed with her. When I had mistakenly thought Ares had stepped into my place, I had been sad at the thought that I was no longer needed, but I had also been happy that my sister had comrades she could speak more freely with. Sadly, that had all been a misunderstanding.

Ruti did have proper friends now in Tisse and Mister Crawly Wawly. And I couldn't have been happier about that.

"In truth, this is something that Ruti should be telling you herself, Gideon… No, I'll call you Red, as well. However, the current situation makes it a bit difficult for her to be able to do that," Tisse prefaced.

"I understand. It's fine."

Both Rit and I had already realized that something was going on with Ruti. She had never been as expressive, smiling and crying and all that, as she had been lately. And more than anything else, she would never have been able to say she was going to live here in Zoltan with the impulses of her blessing eating at her.

"I trust the two of you, so I'll share everything I know."

Tisse carefully conveyed everything that she had seen and heard. I couldn't hide my surprise that the effects of the incident here in Zoltan had reached Ruti so far away. Zoltan was supposed to be a backwater far removed from the battle with the demon lord's army.

"I never would have thought that contract demon would make a pact with Ruti."

Tisse did not know what the contract demon had talked with Ruti about, either. Ruti had captured the creature and interrogated it by herself.

"That was how she learned the effects of Devil's Blessing and the recipe to prepare it."

"Red, can Ruti not just use that medicine you gave Ademi?" Rit asked.

"No, it wouldn't have any effect on her."

The medicine I had given Ademi to tamp down his blessing's impulses was considered a poison. Ruti had Immunity to Poison, meaning it would have no effect.

The reason I had researched that medicine in the first place was that I had wanted to find a way to free Ruti from the pressures of her blessing, at least temporarily.

"If she keeps using Devil's Blessing to suppress her own, what do you think will happen?" Tisse asked, deep in thought.

If she just kept taking it, huh… The image of one of the people who had overdosed on the Devil's Blessing morphed into Ruti in my head.

"I don't know the principle behind how the Devil's Blessing works, so I can't say for sure, but I suspect that as long as the immunities from the Hero blessing remain, she will be fine. But the drug is supposed to lower the user's innate blessing level."

"So the symptoms of overdosing will show up once she drops enough levels to lose her immunity?" Tisse reasoned.

"That seems most likely."

I'd seen the symptoms of several dozen overdoses at Dr. Newman's clinic.

Devil's Blessing was incredibly addictive, and when it was taken in excessive quantities, it could lead to intense headaches and cardio-pulmonary arrest. But those symptoms had only been observed in people with low levels.

In addition, overconsumption could also lead to abnormalities in body functions, like a typical anesthetic. However, for people with a sufficiently high blessing level, the medicine's physical properties were outstripped by the vitality and recovery effects brought about by the blessing.

Things became complicated because Devil's Blessing also lowered the user's blessing level, but even still, as the ax demon blessing grew in level, it became possible to endure the symptoms of overdosing in the same way when that blessing became sufficiently high, too. Other than the dependence and the murderous impulses associated with the ax demon blessing gaining strength, it shouldn't cause Ruti any physical problems...

"Wait a minute," I said.

"What is it?" Rit sounded uneasy when she saw my expression suddenly shift.

"I don't know all the details of preparation, but doesn't that drug require a demon's heart?"

"That would be tough for most people to acquire, but it shouldn't be a problem for Ruti."

She was more than strong enough to attack one of the demon lord's army's camps and gather dozens of hearts. Zoltan was far from the war, however.

"The recipe Ruti is using doesn't require demon hearts," Tisse chimed in.

Wait. What? Devil's Blessing is a medicine that uses a demon's bless-ing to quell the impulses of the imbiber's innate one, right?

"How would it suppress urges without the demon heart at the crux of it all?" I questioned.

All three of us fell silent as we struggled to grasp the possibility of such a thing.

As adventurers, we all had a certain amount of knowledge regarding medicines. I was the only one who made remedies, but Rit and Tisse still understood more than the average apothecary. Without all that knowledge, the two likely would have fallen in battle long before this point. Precisely because of that, they could recognize the contradic-tion implicit in the medicine Ruti was taking.

"What does that mean? It was a demon that made that medicine. It went so far as to kill fellow demons to create it. If it was possible to craft without resorting to such methods, why even bother going through all that in the first place?" I wondered.

"It's unnatural. I'm sorry; I should have paid closer attention," Tisse apologized. It was understandable that she hadn't noticed at the time, though. Up until she had arrived in Zoltan, she'd thought the medicine was for defeating the demon lord. She'd had no way of knowing that Ruti's goal was to suppress the Hero blessing's impulses with Devil's Blessing.

"…Tisse, you're an assassin who joined the party because Ares hired you, right? Are you sure you want to get involved in this?"

"Accompanying Ruti is in line with the contract."

Tisse did not seem to have any strong opinions about the possibility that Ruti might abandon her quest to defeat the demon lord. Maybe it wasn't even that big a deal to her because slaying the demon lord had never been her goal.

Regardless, what was important was that Tisse was a far better friend for Ruti than I had first suspected. I could feel myself tearing up, but since we were in the middle of discussing something this serious, I kept it to a silent feeling of gratitude.

"I think there's something fundamentally wrong with the idea of making a single person shoulder the fate of a world with however many millions and tens of millions of people living in it," Rit stated.

She had said almost the same thing when she had first met the Hero's party. It was because she felt that way that she had refused our assistance and tried to protect Loggervia herself.

"But just thinking that isn't enough." Rit's expression was clouded over.

In the end, it had been Ruti who had saved Loggervia. If the Hero hadn't been there, Rit's kingdom would have suffered the same tragedy that had befallen the many other cities occupied by the demon lord's forces.

"Whether Ruti decides to continue fighting the demon lord is something that she should decide for herself."

"…You're right, Tisse. Discussions about the fate of the world can wait until after Ruti figures out what she wants."

"Yeah. Everyone in the Hero's party joined of our own volition. The king gave neither Ares nor I orders. I did it to fight alongside my sister, and Ares did it to restore his family's honor. Theodora joined to save the world with her martial prowess, which is why she had stepped down from her position as a spear-wielding instructor with the temple knights. Danan came on to avenge his hometown after it was razed by demons. Yarandrala joined out of a sense of righteousness. We all chose to be there, all except Ruti. Her blessing forced her into all of this."

I recalled the faces of those I had battled beside.

There had been others, too, who had fought with the Hero's party for a time. Two soldiers had accompanied us on their lord's orders, and a priest from the holy church in the capital had traveled with us as an observer. None of them had remained for very long, however. Whatever status or power the person giving the orders had, it was a difficult thing to continue risking your life on the front lines of the battle against the demon lord's forces rampaging across the continent for no reason other than you were told to. Leaving became an even more enticing prospect when the adventure saddled you with enough treasure to live a life of luxury countless times over.

"In that sense, I'm not a comrade. I'm merely accompanying her as part of a job request taken by the Assassins Guild," Tisse said.

"That's not true at all," I cut in, stopping her there. "If you were only doing your job, you wouldn't be here. You're here discussing how to save the Hero with us because you want to, right?"

Mister Crawly Wawly's leg snapped up at that.

"Right, Mister Crawly Wawly isn't here because I commanded him, either." Tisse nodded as she smiled at her spider.

"Saving the Hero... The truth is: I've looked for a way to do that before," I admitted, earning serious looks from Rit and Tisse.

I had searched for a way to suppress blessing urges during the breaks in our journey. The medicine I had given Ademi was one of the fruits of that effort, and the advice I had given Al when he was worried about his blessing was another.

The trouble was, the Hero blessing granted the ultimate power in exchange for equally overwhelming impulses. One time, when I had infiltrated a wild elf settlement, I had gotten a chance to speak with an elder there. I asked her for help, and I still remember very clearly what she said in reply.

You wish to suppress the impulses of the Hero? There is no way, save death.

To the best of my knowledge, restraining a blessing that powerful was impossible, even for the wild elves, those said to have the most profound understanding of blessings of anyone on Avalon.

"I'll make some fresh tea."

It was a problem with seemingly no way out. We were just going to have to take our time talking it over. But while I hadn't been able to solve the problem by myself before, this time I had Rit and Tisse and Mister Crawly Wawly. I believed that we would find a way to save Ruti.

✳   ✳   ✳

"I guess we don't have any choice but to ask that alchemist for more details."

All our conversation succeeded in doing was making it clear that Tisse, Rit, and I knew too little about Devil's Blessing.

"Not that there's any saying how much Godwin understands about Devil's Blessing, either."

Still, he was the man who'd been taught the recipe directly from a contract demon. That had to make him the closest thing Zoltan had to an expert on the drug.

"Ummm…" Tisse raised her hand. She almost seemed a little bit scared. I wondered what could trouble her so. "Regarding Ruti breaking Godwin out of prison, are you upset with her about that?"

"Oh, that?"

Ahhh, yeah, I definitely look like that kind of person.

"First of all, hmmm, well, Ruti shared how she really feels, so I guess I should come clean, too."

"Come clean?"

"I'm not the sort of guy who would go risking my life for some random person I don't know and have never met."

"Huh? But you were in the Hero's party…"

"I only joined because Ruti was the Hero. I mean, if it was for a friend or the people in this part of Zoltan, then yeah, I could fight, but beyond that, I don't really care enough to be risking my life over it."

"That's surprising. I had heard stories about the second in command of the Bahamut Knights fighting countless monsters and saving many people," Tisse said.

"That was because I kept asking for the sorts of missions where powerful monsters were likely to appear to raise my level as much as possible for when Ruti would set out on her journey. I focused on that, and before I knew it, I had risen through the ranks."

"Is that so…"

If I didn't feel that way, I wouldn't have holed up here in Zoltan and set my sights on a quiet life like this.

"Only a few prisoners and guards got hurt, right? I'm not going to say it was a good thing, but I don't think berating you two over it is worthwhile, either."

Tisse seemed genuinely shocked to hear me say that so easily.

"And I'm the terrible princess who ran away from the castle to work as an adventurer and bodyguard," Rit reminded with a wry chuckle.

Rit loved her homeland, but she didn't have an absolutist stance about following the law by any means, either. As far as we were concerned, we didn't have anything to scold Ruti for when it came to the prison break.

"In that case, please make that clear to Ruti if you get a chance. She is probably scared of you finding out," requested Tisse.

"Got it."

Rit and I nodded with smiles. Ruti really had found herself a great friend.

"Back to the task at hand, Godwin's our best bet at determining a course of action. You said he's in the elf ruins where I go to gather medicinal herbs, right?"

"Ruti destroyed the lift system, so you can't get down without dripping over one hundred meters."

"A classic Ruti brute-force solution."

With that, there wouldn't be any other people getting in. Ruti had destroyed the elevator, but I could use the Acrobatics mastery Slow Fall, and Rit could either make do somehow with her spirit magic, or I could hold on to her while I descended. And judging by the fact that Tisse wasn't saying anything, she probably had her own way to get down, too.

"Looks like that won't be a problem for us."

"Yes."

Our plan was set. It was a perfect time to act since Ruti was in the ruins right now.

"Let's close up shop for the day and head there," I declared as I stood up.

"Ah, wait," Rit interjected, as if she suddenly remembered something.

"What is it?"

"Isn't today when that merchant ship comes? I was thinking of getting some alchemy tools to analyze Devil's Blessing."

"Godwin mentioned not having the right tools as well," added Tisse. "We gathered all those we could find in Zoltan, but the selection here wasn't particularly great."

"Even so, this is the last stop for the merchant ship. Do we really still think they have what we need?"

Zoltan was in the middle of nowhere. The merchant ships coming from the west turned around at Zoltan and began return routes. There wasn't much profit to be made out here, so the only vessels that actually docked in town were smaller ones that were cheaper to crew. There was no telling whether they would even have what we were looking for.

"Even so, the ships only come once or twice a month, so wouldn't it be better to at least check today while we can?"

"Fair enough. In that case, I'll go check out the harbor. I can run faster than a horse or a riding drake," I said.

"Very well. I have a note with the tools that Godwin said he needed." Tisse pulled a memo and a bag of silver coins out of her item box. There were several expensive tools—Arphilia filters and things like that—listed on the note. It would be hard to buy all of that with the cash I had available, so I gratefully accepted the money from Tisse.

"All right, we're going to rent some riding drakes and head out," Rit declared.

"Got it. I'll be along right behind you," I replied.

We changed into travel gear, and when we left, I flipped the sign on the front door to the side that read CLOSED FOR THE DAY.

*   *   *

The harbor district was on the west side of Zoltan, edged up against the river.

As the name on the map implied, you could find the docks there. That said, it wasn't some great ocean-side pier, just a small jetty on the side of a river. This kept the large ships from entering. It was mostly small sailing ships and galleys with shallow drafts.

Zoltan got its fair share of storms, and sailing up to the harbor in the summer was dangerous. That was part of why Zoltan was so disconnected from the rest of the world.

There were three new vessels in the harbor, an unusual sight out here.

"It's always just the one normally."

The ships that usually moored in Zoltan's harbor were rowboats that went upriver to trade with the nearby villages, fishing boats, and the three caravel sailing ships that could hold twenty people and made up the total of the Zoltan navy.

While every other country was using new model galleons or big, sturdy galleys, having a trio of old caravels to guard against an attack by water seemed unreliable. Not that there was anyone to be warring with out here.

Given that, though, it was not particularly difficult to tell when new ships had arrived. In addition to a regular merchant ship, there were also two clippers in the harbor. One was a small galley, and the other was a midsize sloop. The latter had laid up anchor in the middle of the river, maybe concerned about its draft being too deep and running aground. It was using boats to ferry back and forth into the harbor.

"That smaller ship is maybe a delivery for some rich person in the central district? And the midsize one looks like it might be headed east beyond the Wall at the End of the World?"

If so, then they were probably selling rare things in the harbor to earn some pocket change. There was no saying whether they had alchemy tools, but it was worth knowing for sure.

Getting a little bit excited, I started walking to the harbor marketplace.

✻   ✻   ✻

"Two days late? That's sufficient, I suppose."

"Heh-heh, apologies, Chief."

It was a chartered ship to deliver items that had been requested as soon as possible.

Captain Blake of the light galley *Goldenroad* lowered his head apologetically.

But in his mind, he felt like spitting. There weren't storms on the seas around these parts in winter, but the wind and waves were strong, making it incredibly difficult to navigate. And sometimes, the breeze would just disappear all of a sudden, so even a tried-and-true seaman like Blake couldn't always accurately estimate the time a ship would make on those seas.

Damn landlubbers.

But not even the slightest trace of it showed in his expression. He just forced his tanned face into a friendly grin and apologized. Blake was a sailor, but his blessing was Court Bard.

Negotiations were right in his wheelhouse, whether he needed to soothe his clients, anger them, or anything in between. Still, he did not feel like using any of his emotional manipulation skills on the man before him. The young client stroked his chin as he glanced through the registry with a smile pasted across his face.

"So then, can you show me the items?"

"Aye, aye."

Maybe it was the self-confidence that the powerful exuded, but Blake could tell that the customer he was dealing with was strong. Simultaneously, though, there were warning bells in the back of his mind saying this young man was not to be trusted.

"Your items have been offloaded into the warehouse next to the ship, Mr. Bui, so if you will."

The man named Bui was holding the registry in his left hand as he stroked his chin with his right. All of a sudden, a grim look crossed his face.

"Is something wrong?"

Bui was staring at someone who appeared to be an adventurer with a bronze sword hanging at his waist. He looked like a normal, run-of-the-mill quest taker to Blake.

"Just a fellow I don't really enjoy dealing with. If possible, I'd prefer not to speak with him," Bui replied with a shrug.

He lowered his voice as he started counting the items that had been delivered.

I've got the tools together to carry out the investigation…if only I could find someone of sufficient ability to help…

Bui picked up the cutting-edge investigation gear he had requested as he pondered what to do about a helper.

✳   ✳   ✳

Several hours later, two men and a woman climbed out of a small boat and stretched as they stepped onto dry land.

"What a shabby harbor," Ares muttered to himself as he looked around Zoltan's docks. Usually, Ares would have been able to keep that much to himself, but he was currently at his limit.

A sense of unease and irritation was consuming him. He needed to find the Hero, Ruti, and be at her side when she defeated the demon lord. If he failed in that, what would have been the point of his having continued to journey through all that blood and mud?

Hearing his comment, Theodora furrowed her brow slightly. But if she started getting into it with him over everything, they would not even manage to find lodging for the day.

"Are you okay?"

"Yes, ma'am."

Albert was staggering along behind Theodora. Because he was an escaped prisoner in Zoltan, Albert had wrapped bandages around his face to hide his identity. The bindings were a magic item that made people unable to focus on whoever used them to conceal themselves. Of course, to Ares and Theodora and other people at the level of the Hero's party, a perceived disruption of that tier would have no effect.

Still, Theodora expected that no one living out in Zoltan would be able to see through it.

"Despite the facilities, it's quite lively."

"Because a merchant ship is moored. The market is probably open. The crew of the vessel we took seemed to be planning on doing some trading while we are in the port, too."

The *Sylphid* that Ares had paid so much to borrow was not usually provisioned with anything more than food and water. However, the sailors would use their pay to buy small but valuable items like precious metals and handicrafts in settlements they visited and then sell them in other locations.

Anything bought in a backwater like Zoltan was unlikely to go for a high price, though.

"It's fortunate we didn't end up having to go around the Wall at the End of the World. The *Sylphid*'s sailors were not really interested in trying to cross that route," Theodora said with a sigh.

Ares had gotten the crew of the *Sylphid* to agree to ferry him anywhere he wanted, but the sailors had undoubtedly never imagined that Ares would insist on going around the Wall at the End of the World.

There were no reliable stops for resupplying past Zoltan. It would have been rough sailing for a single high-speed ship. They had already begun planning to borrow several more boats and sail out at the head of a fleet if it had ended up coming to that.

But as they had approached Zoltan, they'd realized that the Hero was not actually on the other side of the Wall at the End of the World but in Zoltan itself.

"Crossing those peaks would've been a simple matter for that airship, but by sea or by land, it is quite difficult."

If trade had been possible with those beyond the Wall at the End of the World, Zoltan would not still be such a Podunk.

As things currently stood, the only ways to trade with the eastern lands beyond the mountainous barrier were to take the crown passage around the north side or the dragon path through the mountains.

Either option was incredibly harsh, and it was estimated that over half of those who attempted one of the journeys lost their lives.

Despite Zoltan's harbor's size and appearance, it was still filled with the usual back-and-forth from sailors shouting out to one another from time to time.

"I'm tellin' ya. This one-armed martial artist beat the crap outta them pirates!"

"Quit pullin' my leg! How could one son of a bitch take out five whole raider ships?"

"He just freakin' punched the boat, and it split in two!"

"Ga-ha-ha-ha! If you're gonna tell tall tales, at least make 'em more believable, ya drunk louts!"

"The hell'd you say?!"

"Ain't no damn hundred-man pirate ship that'd break from a single punch!"

"I saw it with my own eyes! He smashed the entire goddamn ship to pieces!"

Ares's scowl deepened the more he heard the shouts from around the merchant ship.

"Let's hurry and get an inn. I would like to be done in this filthy little town as soon as possible. The downtown is apparently at least marginally less dreadful, so let's look for a place there."

"I'll be getting an inn here. You can gather information better in a port."

"Do as you please. We already know where Ruti is, though, so there's not much point in asking around now." Ares squared his shoulders and left with a snort.

"He's normally not that harsh," Theodora said apologetically to Albert.

Ares had never possessed a kind personality, but he wasn't usually so short-tempered, either.

"He's kept on the journey all this time because his family has lost all its prestige, land, and wealth. His hope is to restore the Srowa name to its former status," Theodora explained.

Albert shook his head to indicate he did not mind. "Is it really that difficult to restore his family's honor?" he asked.

"Four generations ago, the head of the Srowa family led a rebellion. There was even foreign intrigue with a country looking to annex some of the nation's territory. It was high treason. The Srowa patriarch attempted to kill the king and claim the country for himself while negotiating a deal to cede land to a foreign power. Most of the Srowa family was executed. Ares's grandfather happened to have been studying at the estate of a different family, which is how the lineage survived."

"…That's quite the past."

"You'd do best not to speak of it in front of Ares. He apparently can't forgive the fact that he has suffered so much because of his lineage's history."

"I won't mention it," Albert said, nodding.

For the prideful Ares, it was a terrible legacy to bear. The subject was not one to be broached lightly.

Albert tucked what he had heard deep in his heart as he led Theodora to an inn in the harbor district.

*   *   *

After Bui had finished verifying his shipment, he'd left instructions for the various tools to be delivered to the mansion he was renting.

At roughly the same time, Red was looking around the market stalls erected near the merchant ship.

"Oh! They actually have it."

I paid in silver and collected several different tools.

They hadn't had everything, but I had at least been able to get the instruments for precise measurements as well as filters and other alchemy tools. I now had all the most important items on Tisse's list.

"Even just this much cost over a thousand payril, though."

During my tenure with the Bahamut Knights and the Hero's party, I wouldn't have blinked at a bill like that, but it was quite a lot of money for me now. There weren't any loans or tabs when dealing with the merchant ships, either. You had to pay the full price up front.

Carefully packing away the things I had purchased, I stood and got ready to catch up with Rit and Tisse.

"Gideon!"

Suddenly, I heard a booming shout. It was a voice I knew well. But why was he here?

A giant shadow leaped over the crowd's heads with a nimbleness belying its owner's size. There was a "*Thud!*" as a huge man stood in my path.

"It really is you, Gideon! That's some shabby gear you've got there!" He grabbed my shoulder without any consideration for my circumstances.

Why now of all times…?

"Cool it a bit there, Danan. We stand out here, so let's head someplace a little quieter. I'm sure we've both got things to talk about."

Danan had lost his right arm from his elbow down since I had seen him last, but from the way he grinned, it didn't appear that he minded at all.

"I'm so glad I could see you again, pal!"

It seemed like this was going to be a bit of a hassle. I would never have guessed I would run into Danan again here and now.

It was probably a mistake, but seeing how happily Danan was beaming at meeting me again, I couldn't bring myself to give him the cold shoulder.

"Yeah… I guess I'm glad, too."

Internally, I was at my wit's end about what to do…but I was also happy to see an old comrade again.

✳   ✳   ✳

The harbor district was hit by storms often. It also wasn't all that rare for a building to be washed away in the customary annual flooding when the river rose. The people who lived there had given up on winning against the weather. As a result, the harbor district had developed a construction style that consisted of simple buildings that were easy to rebuild when storms or floods destroyed them.

The place Danan and I shifted to was in a quiet part of the neighborhood without many people around. It had been half demolished in a hurricane three years back. The walls were a patchwork of old and new, and the wind could be heard whistling through crevices.

The owner was a hunched old lady who took our orders with a friendly smile.

"Here's your fish soup."

"Thank you."

She set two big bowls of broth with pieces of fish meat floating in them on the counter, and I carried them over to our table. It was a little late for lunch, so Danan and I were the only customers in the shop.

"This looks delicious!" Danan declared as his eyes gleamed in anticipation.

"Don't you just say that for everything?"

I smiled, seeing him like that. That was Danan's go-to line whenever he had food in front of him. Any halfway decent meal received his excited appraisal. I couldn't help feeling nostalgic witnessing that habit of his again after so long.

"Nah, after you left, I haven't been able to say that nearly as much. The food we ate on the road went to shit after that."

"Don't talk about shit when we're eating. Did you switch to a rotation for preparing the meals?"

"No, Ares said he'd do it, so we left it to him."

"Ah, no wonder, then."

That sounded like Ares didn't know much about cooking. I guess he had said he'd do the stuff I was taking care of when he pushed me out. But it was unreasonable for him to do all that alone.

"Leaving the responsibility to just one guy who can't do it is a recipe for frustration. You've got to trade it off some. Offer to share the load since it isn't easy or something. If you do that, you can talk things through with everyone about how to improve. You might even discover someone has a hidden talent."

"Sure, but the only thing we're good at is fighting," Danan said as he scratched his head. "It's all because you up and disappeared out of nowhere."

Danan's arm became a blur. The next moment, his finger was right in front of my forehead. I tilted my neck, just barely evading his flick.

"Looks like you haven't gotten too rusty," Danan observed with a grin as he pulled his arm back.

That was no joke. A flick from those giant fingers would've been sore for three days.

I was lucky enough to evade it, but Danan's movements had gotten quite a bit sharper since I'd last seen him. And that was him playing around. It was scary to imagine just how much he had grown.

"You can count the number of people in this world who can dodge my flick on just two hands."

"Nah, I can tell the difference in strength. You're strong, Danan."

Even when we were traveling together, he'd been more powerful than me, and that gap had only widened with time. While I was taking it easy here in Zoltan, Danan had been fighting on the front lines against the demon lord's army, surviving countless do-or-die situations.

A high level was my only redeeming quality, so once he had opened a gap with me in level, too, I had no chance left of winning.

Danan seemed almost sad when he heard me say that.

"…That's not how it feels to me, Gideon. I think you're a man who's truly worthy of respect."

Danan and I slurped the soup down without worrying about manners. It was simple enough, just the fish and salt for flavor. There were chunks of potato and some cabbage floating in it, too.

Although it contained nothing special, it still tasted good. With a low Cooking skill, it was best to simply use the flavors of the ingredients themselves. The fish soup was a good meal that stayed faithful to that principle.

The old lady who ran the store had apparently been a singer for the sailors in the past. After retiring, she switched to an entirely different job and became the proprietress of this tavern, coming up with all sorts of ideas and using her natural smile to keep the pub running all these years despite not having skills suited to it.

"So why are you here?" Danan finally asked.

"…You heard from Ares, right? I ran away."

I had asked Ares to coordinate a story with me to avoid causing problems for the Bahamut Knights, but Tisse and Ruti had told me that he'd spilled the beans the second he'd been pressed on the matter. I'm sure Danan knew that much, too.

"Because Ares told you to leave?"

"That was part of it…but it was also because I had recognized it myself. I could feel it acutely in the battle with Desmond of the Earth. I couldn't keep up with the fighting any further beyond that."

"That's not true!" Danan slammed his fist down on the table. The soup sloshed, spilling out a bit.

"I didn't fully understand it until after you'd left, but you're a strong guy, Gideon. I'm not just talking about physical might, either. I mean the courage to make calm judgments when fighting someone stronger than you and the knowledge to make the most effective moves on a battlefield even without martial arts or magic. You are a genuinely capable man, and you were crucial to our journey." Danan's eyes were serious…but I had already made my decision, and I couldn't simply stay here answering questions forever.

"I'm sorry, but I've already found my home here. I can't travel with you anymore."

"How are you going to protect that home if we don't defeat the demon lord?!"

"You have a point."

Danan immediately honed in on the problem. Albert's words ran through my mind.

Those with strength have a responsibility to wield it.

Was it a sin for me not to fight? Did we have a responsibility to battle if the Divine Blessings we received at birth wished us to do so? Watching Ruti all her life had often left me wondering that question.

That little girl had been forced at birth to bear the responsibility of saving the world. If she said that she didn't want to fight, neither the people nor her blessing would ever forgive her.

Did the person bearing the Hero blessing really have to sacrifice their life for the sake of being the Hero?

No! Our blessings aren't supposed to govern us. We have our own dreams and our own lives!

Wasn't it evident that I had the freedom to choose to live my life how I pleased? And that Ruti would have the same? I wouldn't yield that one point. I'd even argue that to God's face.

Danan and I stared each other down for a while, but in the end, Danan looked away first.

"…Hah, well, I guess you stopped of your own will."

"Ares was the impetus, but I *chose* to quit."

There was a moment's silence between us. There were mixed emotions in our eyes as we looked at each other.

"I don't understand it, but fine. I think I'll learn a little about what you've been up to here and then decide on what I'll do next."

"I don't mind that…but there's one other problem."

"What's that?"

"Ruti's here, too."

"Huh?" Danan froze in shock. "Why's the Hero here?"

"…If you heard the reason, you might get mad at her."

"Me? Mad at her? There's no way."

Should I tell him the truth? I was sure I could talk my way around it and avoid mentioning Ruti's problem, but…

"Danan, I'm going to tell you everything I know. You're Ruti's comrade. You deserve to know the suffering she's endured."

"The Hero was suffering?"

Why had the Hero's party gotten so out of sorts after I left? When I'd first heard that things had fallen apart, I couldn't understand it. The tasks I had done for the party were just a collection of routine chores that didn't require any skills. To put it bluntly, anyone could have accomplished them with some effort.

My absence was always going to cause a little difficulty, but I hadn't been doing anything the other party members couldn't have taken care of if they'd spread the load around.

However, Ares had tried to do it all himself, resulting in things falling apart. Everyone had grown more and more dissatisfied, and the party had started to collapse.

So was Ares the root cause? He was undoubtedly part of it. If he had only asked for some assistance, it wouldn't have ended up like this. Still, it was more than that. Ares may have volunteered to take on all my responsibilities alone while not being able, but no one else had offered to help.

I guess you could also assert that it was because our other companions had stopped trusting Ares after he'd pushed me out. The reason Yarandrala and Danan had left was that they didn't have faith in Ares.

"A true comrade, huh."

Ironically, what Ares had said to me back then was probably the root cause of the party's collapse.

"You're a true comrade as far as I'm concerned," Danan said.

It was nice that he felt that way. I was glad, really. But that wasn't what I meant.

I explained to Danan about how Ruti was constantly tormented and pushed by the Hero blessing. He listened as I outlined the way Ruti had lost so much of her humanity to the immunities her blessing gave her. I also informed him of her using Devil's Blessing to suppress urges and how she might walk away from being the Hero.

The comrades who had been together with Ruti for so long had not been able to understand her anguish. Ruti was the Hero tasked with leading the party. She only held that status because of her blessing. If everyone had followed the roles their blessings gave them obediently, the party would have naturally come together. That was probably what Ares had meant by a true comrade.

However, it hadn't worked out that smoothly because we weren't slaves to our blessing.

"Suffering because of your blessing? I hadn't ever thought of it like that." My words were a genuine surprise to Danan. "The Martial Artist blessing fits me like a glove. It's fun to train myself, and I get excited about fighting powerful enemies. The feeling of getting stronger is just satisfying beyond belief. I could endure any hardship for that sensation… That's just the kind of guy I am."

"Yeah."

"…I don't get it. I just don't get it."

Danan was one of the people who couldn't comprehend the concept of suffering because of one's blessing's urges. I had never met anyone as loved by their blessing as Danan. The fact that he was more powerful than a Crusader and Sage despite the Martial Artist blessing being rather plain was proof of that.

"I don't get it, but I do at least get that there are a lot of things I don't get! So all I can do is just fight!"

"Look at this musclehead."

"All I can do is battle. If the Hero wants something, I'll fight for it! And if the Hero decides to quit, I'll think about what to do when that time comes!"

Sheesh. Danan hasn't changed at all.

"With that settled, we don't have time to be screwing around here! Let's go, Gideon! If the Hero is suffering, then it's our job to help her out!"

"Wait, wait, wait. We covered my stuff, but what about you?"

"We can walk and talk. There's nothing that special to say about me!"

I would have thought losing your right arm is a pretty big deal…but it was clear from Danan's face that he was not in the mood to just sit around.

"Got it."

It had been a long time since I had seen that side of Danan—the loveable musclehead who always acted before thinking. He was the sort of man who would never stop and worry, no matter the situation. From time to time, that simplicity of his felt almost blindingly radiant.

✳   ✳   ✳

The door opened, and Red and Danan hurried outside.

"Is it okay not to follow them?"

Albert was sitting in a seat far away from them, bandages still wrapped around his face. Theodora had her spear on her back as she stared down at her hands resting on the table, speechless.

Theodora possessed the greatest clerical magic in the world. If she was serious about it, then as long as neither of them bore any hostility, even Danan and Red would have trouble noticing her and Albert through her concealment magic.

Milady is going to walk away from the quest to slay the demon lord?

Theodora was not capable of viewing things as straightforwardly as Danan. She was lost in anxious thoughts about what to do next, not even aware of Albert nervously peeking over at her.

On an emotional level, Theodora wanted to help Ruti and Gideon. If Ruti, of all people, was in pain, then she wished to aid her!

Theodora had never regretted her inability to see the world as simplistically as Danan as much as she did that day.

Epilogue

- - - - - - - - -

The Sage's Decision

Ares removed his gear, staggered over to the bed, and threw himself down on it.

"Hmph."

Honestly, he would have liked to start chasing after Ruti immediately, but he was exhausted from using his magic for days and nights on end.

I don't know whether this is some villainous plot to impede my aspirations, but either way, my victory in the end is assured.

That Ares had procured a way of tracking the Hero across the world was proof enough of that. The Sage's mouth warped into a grin.

There was a knock on the door.

"Who is it?" Ares tiresomely pushed himself up. "I said 'Who is it?' I do not wish to be disturbed."

"It's me."

Ares recognized the voice, but its owner should not have been in Zoltan. On his guard, Ares stood. He kept his right hand free to use magic at any moment as he slowly approached the door.

"Are you sure you don't have the wrong room?" Ares asked, playing dumb.

"No, I came here to meet Ares the Sage. It's me, Danan."

Slowly, Ares opened the door. A large, muscular man was standing there.

"Long time no see." Danan was holding a bag of sugared fruits in *both hands* and grinning.

"Come on, these oranges are great."

"..."

Danan held out the bag for Ares as he entered the room.

"From the look of it, you're pretty busted up. Sugared fruit does wonders for fatigue."

Ares formed a sign with his right hand, activating a spell to check for poison. He confirmed that there was no toxin anywhere inside the sack.

"Always so careful." Danan smiled wryly, but he did not seem to mind the excessive caution. Ares took one of the oranges from the bag and put it into his mouth.

"Hmph." He could sense that there might be something to the idea that sugars suited a tired body well, but he maintained his visible displeasure to antagonize Danan. Seeing that, Danan grimaced.

"If it so pleases your palate..."

"Why are you here, Danan?"

"Me? Because I was searching for Gideon. I got some information that he was in these parts. I could ask you the same thing, though. Never would have pegged running into you in this backwater—and by yourself even. Where's the Hero?"

"Gideon is here?" Ares cut in.

"Yeah, he's running an apothecary in town."

For just a moment, the suspicion that this might have been a plot by Gideon crossed Ares's mind. But he immediately rejected that idea as too absurd. There was no way someone with a blessing as worthless as Gideon's could devise something so devious.

Nonetheless, Ares felt a growing anger over the possibility that Gideon might be interfering with his aspirations. Danan's eyes narrowed slightly after noticing this.

"So where is the Hero?" the bear of a man asked again.

"...She isn't here."

"What do you mean?"

"There's no need to explain it to you."

"I mean, Gideon's here, too. She deserves to know that."

Ares's mouth twitched nervously. Danan put his hand to his chin in contemplation.

"Look, just let me know what's going on. It's not like I'm inherently against you, you know. Depending on the situation, I can always keep that bit about Gideon from the Hero."

"…What are you getting at?" Ares pressed, suspicion evident.

"Our goal is to defeat the demon lord, not reunite Gideon and the Hero. Gideon has every intention to stay settled here. He's not thinking about defeating the demon lord anymore. You remember Rizlet of Loggervia, right? He shacked up with her."

"Hmph, so that's the sort of fellow he really is, huh? Running away to live in peace and plotting to marry into royalty while I continue to risk my neck?! How low can one man be!" Ares shrieked.

Danan could not help being shocked by the outburst. It was a pretty shameless thing for the guy who had kicked Gideon out of the party to say.

Though that is precisely why we were able to meet like this. The Asura in Danan's form smirked to itself.

"Anyway, the point is that it would be a waste of time for the Hero to hang around here trying to get him to come back. And I'd rather not waste my time, either. I don't have any desire to be stuck here while she tries to persuade Gideon."

"I see… A rather sensible thought for you."

"I'm the sort of guy who says what I think. But what I say in the moment and what I say when I've had time to calm down and think things through are different."

"That *is* rather like you." Ares smirked in contempt, feeling a secret sense of superiority. Danan was an inferior man, incapable of controlling his emotions.

"Anyway, that's how things are on my end. So why is the Hero here? It's not like she knew Gideon was living in Zoltan, right?"

"…"

"What is it?"

Ares seemed to be pondering whether to answer.

This is… Did he screw up or something? He looks like he's hesitating out of reluctance to say something embarrassing…

Danan could not help but feel exasperated over how foolish Ares was. Hiding what he knew wouldn't accomplish anything. Regardless, Danan decided to probe in a different way.

"Whatever you're going to try, you should do it quickly. Gideon—he's going by the name Red here—is pretty well-known around Zoltan."

"Hmph, in a place like this with such low levels, even someone like him can play at being a big shot?"

In truth, Red was famous for living together with Rit, but Danan did not feel the need to correct Ares on that point.

"Point being, it's entirely possible that the Hero could recognize that Red and Gideon are the same person. If you're here in Zoltan for a reason, you should take care of it quickly. Since I've been here longer, I know a bit about the lay of the land, so I can lend you a hand if you want."

That was Danan's—or rather Shisandan in the form of Danan—offer to Ares.

The demon's goal was to find the object sealed by the wood elves before their downfall and take it back with him.

He had taken the risk of making contact with Ares because he understood what the Sage was after and thus knew that it bore no relation to his goal. Because of that, Shisandan wanted to get Ares and his band as far away from Zoltan as possible, even if that meant helping them.

There were three things that Shisandan was concerned about.

The first was the possibility of the Hero using Devil's Blessing to enhance her battle strength. Particularly if the humans learned that a demon's heart was not a necessary ingredient, even if that happened, taking that medicine was an act of rejection of one's Divine Blessing. It would be viewed as blasphemy by the holy church, and even though the user's innate Divine Blessing was weakened, it would still remain. Considering all those factors, Shisandan felt confident things would not turn out as they had during the era of the ancient elves.

The second thing he feared was the Hero getting her hands on the object he sought. The failure of allowing her to attain the airship would pale in comparison to that falling into her hands.

Most of all, however, Shisandan fretted over the Hero losing her natural blessing to the drug. It should be impossible for modern humans, who lacked all knowledge regarding the essence of Divine Blessings, to achieve what the former True Demon Lord had. If it actually came to that, Shisandan would have to slay the Hero then and there, even if it cost him everything—including his life.

Shisandan was a key general, but he had also been judged to be exceptionally skilled at infiltrating and maneuvering in enemy territory. That was why he had been given such a critical mission.

"…That must be it!" Ares exclaimed, paying no heed to Shisandan. "Ruti realized that Red and Gideon are the same person after speaking with that demon. That was why she came here in the airship!"

Regardless of his conjecture's accuracy, that means the Hero left her comrades behind to come to Zoltan. It seems it truly is unrelated to my mission.

"Danan! Where is Gideon's store?!"

"I mean, I know where it is, but what do you want to do there?"

"Ruti is not here in Zoltan. She's up in the mountains some distance away from here. Doubtless, she will come to meet Gideon soon, so I'm going to command him to disappear before that can happen."

"Command?"

"He's just a normal citizen who has left our party already. He has no choice but to follow my orders!"

"Really? I doubt he'd just obediently listen to you."

"I'll force him to obey by whatever means necessary! Where is his store?!"

He's that irritated over the Hero leaving him behind? Yes, from what I heard in Loggervia, his goal is to restore his family's power. The Hero's party is his one chance… I might be able to make use of him…

Shisandan's lips twisted. If Red had been there, he would surely have realized that it was not really Danan from that expression alone.

"Well, fine, I guess. I'll lead the way."

And if Ares had been in his right mind, he would certainly have noticed that Danan, who had been close with Gideon, would never lead him to Gideon's store after that exchange.

"Kh-ha-ha. Gideon, you bastard…always getting in my way…"

Ares's lips broke into an irregular grin as he clenched his fists so hard that the veins in his hands and arms began to bulge.

Ares's mind was filled with hatred for Gideon, the man who was always in his way.

Afterword

To everyone who has picked up this book, thank you very much! I'm Zappon, the author.

It's because of your support that the story made its way to a third volume. With three books, it starts to take up enough space lined up on a shelf to stand out at a glance. I end up breaking into a grin when I turn around to look at the bookshelf behind me.

I do have one announcement to make: The first volume of the manga adaptation of *Banished from the Hero's Party, I Decided to Live a Quiet Life in the Countryside* is also on sale now!

It's a truly wonderful and adorable manga that shows off lots of Rit's expressions—from angry, to smiling, to blushing, to everything in between. I would love for you to see more of her there!

There is a short story of mine in the manga adaptation. Unlike the winter setting of this book, it's a tale of Rit and Red during the summer, right after their reunion. I tried my best to convey the depth of expression from the manga in my writing, so I suspect those of you who enjoy reading about Red and Rit's relationship will find it pleasing.

All right, let's touch a bit on the contents of this book. This time, the setting is winter in Zoltan.

It's fun to write stories set in the various seasons. Between spring, summer, autumn, and winter, I feel like I would never run out of tales to tell about Red and Rit's quiet life. The scene of the two of them huddled together and watching the snow that is the cover for this book was especially fun to write.

And then Ruti showed up.

The Hero, Ruti, had been suffering since the very first volume, and now she's finally arrived in Zoltan. Whether by chance or by fate and driven by different motives, the members of the Hero's party have gathered in Zoltan where Red, who had been kicked out of the group, was living. In this universe, everyone sees Red as a supporting actor, while his little sister, Ruti, has the leading role.

To Ruti, however, Red is her irreplaceable big brother, not some bit player. That question of how to live your life when what the world expects of you is so different from your own desires is the key theme of this work.

As before, it took the help and support of many people in order for this third volume to reach your hands. I would like to use this space to offer my gratitude.

Every other illustration has been fantastic, but the cover for this volume was even lovelier than the previous ones. The fluttering snow and the glimmer of the setting sun, Red's affectionate expression, and the way Rit's face is red from both the cold and the blissful moment—it's truly priceless! Thank you so much, Yasumo!

And I owe a lot to the designer who managed to fit my incredibly long series title so neatly on the cover without ruining it, too. I imagine it must be a struggle every time. I'm sorry, but thank you so much for making it work!

To the proofreader who went through the manuscript with its typos and the like on every page and corrected it, I'm in your debt, once again. Thank you for all your work!

To the people who printed and bound the books, although I'm writing this before the physical volumes have been made, it is because of your hard work that authors can know the joy of their stories becoming novels. Thank you very much!

Also, to my editor, Miyakawa, who advised me to write a more detailed scene in the snow, helped line things up everywhere along the way so this book could be made and delivered, and so, so many other things; thank you for all that you do!

Lastly, to the readers who picked up this novel, those who have followed the story since it began, those who purchased this because of the manga version, and those who supported the online version, this book would not exist without all of you. Thank you so very much!

Let's meet again in Volume 4!

Zappon
2018, in a town where snow has not yet begun to fall

Hello, this is Yasumo. There were many intricate illustrations this time, but it was still a pleasure to draw them!

The heroes gather on the frontier. Humanity's strongest Sage and the fated brother and sister finally clash?!

"You are not a true comrade."

BANISHED FROM THE HERO'S PARTY,

I Decided to Live a Quiet Life in the Countryside

4

COMING SUMMER 2021!

HAVE YOU BEEN TURNED ON TO LIGHT NOVELS YET?

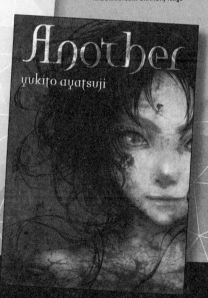